A Book Of

INDUSTRIAL ECONOMICS

M.Com. Part - I : Semester - II
As Per New Syllabus
Effective from June 2013

Mrs. Kiran Jotwani
M.A., B.Ed.
Pune

NIRALI PRAKASHAN
ADVANCEMENT OF KNOWLEDGE

N0249

INDUSTRIAL ECONOMICS (M.Com. Part I : Sem. II)   **ISBN : 978-93-83971-42-8**

Third Edition	:	**January 2016**
©	:	**Author**

Published By :
NIRALI PRAKASHAN
Abhyudaya Pragati, 1312, Shivaji Nagar,
Off J.M. Road, Pune – 411005
Tel - (020) 25512336/37/39, Fax - (020) 25511379
Email : niralipune@pragationline.com

☞ **DISTRIBUTION CENTRES**

PUNE

Nirali Prakashan : 119, Budhwar Peth, Jogeshwari Mandir Lane, Pune 411002, Maharashtra
Tel : (020) 2445 2044, 66022708, Fax : (020) 2445 1538
Email : bookorder@pragationline.com, niralilocal@pragationline.com

Nirali Prakashan : S. No. 28/27, Dhyari, Near Pari Company, Pune 411041
Tel : (020) 24690204 Fax : (020) 24690316
Email : dhyari@pragationline.com, bookorder@pragationline.com

MUMBAI

Nirali Prakashan : 385, S.V.P. Road, Rasdhara Co-op. Hsg. Society Ltd.,
Girgaum, Mumbai 400004, Maharashtra
Tel : (022) 2385 6339 / 2386 9976, Fax : (022) 2386 9976
Email : niralimumbai@pragationline.com

☞ **DISTRIBUTION BRANCHES**

JALGAON

Nirali Prakashan : 34, V. V. Golani Market, Navi Peth, Jalgaon 425001,
Maharashtra, Tel : (0257) 222 0395, Mob : 94234 91860

KOLHAPUR

Nirali Prakashan : New Mahadvar Road, Kedar Plaza, 1st Floor Opp. IDBI Bank
Kolhapur 416 012, Maharashtra. Mob : 9850046155

NAGPUR

Pratibha Book Distributors : Above Maratha Mandir, Shop No. 3, First Floor,
Rani Jhanshi Square, Sitabuldi, Nagpur 440012, Maharashtra
Tel : (0712) 254 7129

DELHI

Nirali Prakashan : 4593/21, Basement, Aggarwal Lane 15, Ansari Road, Daryaganj
Near Times of India Building, New Delhi 110002
Mob : 08505972553

BENGALURU

Pragati Book House : House No. 1, Sanjeevappa Lane, Avenue Road Cross,
Opp. Rice Church, Bengaluru – 560002.
Tel : (080) 64513344, 64513355,Mob : 9880582331, 9845021552
Email:bharatsavla@yahoo.com

CHENNAI

Pragati Books : 9/1, Montieth Road, Behind Taas Mahal, Egmore,
Chennai 600008 Tamil Nadu, Tel : (044) 6518 3535,
Mob : 94440 01782 / 98450 21552 / 98805 82331,
Email : bharatsavla@yahoo.com

niralipune@pragationline.com | www.pragationline.com
Also find us on f www.facebook.com/niralibooks

Preface ...

Business operates in a complex economic, social, political and legal environment which affects its decision-making function. Today, the success of any business depends on quick and effective adjustment with the local, national and international environment.

In fact the whole process of industrialisation is so difficult and complex, for a developing country like India that it taxes a nation's patience, tactfulness and resources. The country was in the past well known for its cottage and small scale industries but in order to industrialise herself, the Industrial Economy of India has undergone rapid changes in recent years.

In this book a comprehensive coverage of the subject is attempted while laying emphasis on highlighting the development that took place during the planning era. This text book has been designed as a self-contained book providing a general introduction to the subject. The book focuses on understanding the behaviour of business firms, when making decisions on location of industrial units and selecting the technique and scale of production. The concepts and tools of economic analysis relevant for business decision-making like theories of location have been discussed at length.

Breaking the traditional approach some new chapters have been included which have a direct bearing on the subject. Today, with industrial development, environment cannot be neglected. This book gives the impact of industrialisation on 'Global Warming'. It also presents the lop-sided development in urbanisation due to industrialisation.

This book has been strictly written as per the new syllabus of Pune University with effect from June 2013. Revision in the syllabus of Industrial Economics makes the application of the subject more fruit-bearing. Students of all levels – graduate and post graduate can take advantage of this comprehensive text book. The topics in the book are arranged in a manner to facilitate easy reading and understanding by the student. Due care has been taken to simplify the language and illustrate the topics with diagrams, wherever needed.

I have quoted, where necessary from the authorities and contemporary writers on the subject, to clarify the points being discussed and acknowledge their thanks.

I am thankful to my friends and long time publisher Shri Dineshbhai Furia, Shri Jignesh Furia and the entire staff of Nirali Prakashan, Pune without whose unerring support and sustained effort, this book would not have seen the light of the day.

I am also thankful to Shri Suresh Jotwani, for his guidance at various stages of this book and in giving live examples to illustrate the subject.

It is hoped that the book will be of great help to the students. Both I and my publishers will be thankful for any suggestions for the improvement of the book. We both are quite confident that this text book will receive the patronage of all for whom it is intended.

Mrs. Kiran Jotwani

Syllabus ...

Contents ...

Chapter **1** ...

Introduction to Industrial Economics

Contents ...

Learning Objectives ...

At the end of the Chapter, you will be able:

* To understand the field of industrial economics

* To be aware of the meaning and scope of industrial economics

* To learn about the inter-relationship between industrial development and economic development

1.1 Introduction

Industrial economics is a distinctive branch of economics which deals with the economic problems of firms and industries, and their relationship with society.

In economic literature it is known by several names such as, 'Economics of Industries', 'Industrial Organisation and Policy', 'Industry and Trade', 'Commerce' and 'Business Economics'.

The name 'Industrial Economics' was adopted in the early 50s' through the writings of P. W. S. Andrews. The two broad elements of industrial economics are:

(i) **Descriptive element**, which deals with the information content of the subject. It aims at providing the industrialists with the information about the competitors, natural resources and factors of production and government rules and regulations related to the concerned industry.

(ii) **Analytical element**, which is concerned with the business policy and decision-making, i.e., dealing with topics such as market analysis, pricing, choice of techniques, location of plant, investment planning, financial decisions, product diversification, hiring and firing of labour and so on.

The two elements are interdependent as only with adequate information one can take proper decisions about any aspect of business.

Industrialisation has a major role to play in the economic development of the underdeveloped countries. It is the only effective answer to the problem of under-development.

By creating large-scale employment opportunities, industrialisation reduces open as well as disguised unemployment in these nations. It brings about economic stability by reducing excessive dependence of the underdeveloped economy of agriculture. At the same time, by introducing technical improvements in agriculture, it also brings about development of the agricultural sector itself. Thus, industrialisation occupies a very important place in the process of economic development of the poor nations.

Industrialisation has been defined by different economists as:

(i) **Eugene Staley** has linked industrialisation with high productivity. According to Staley, *"High productivity produce industrialisation and that industrialisation produce high productivity."*

(ii) **Prof. S. C. Kuchhal** says, *"Industrialisation is also treated as a process in which the economic gains of industrial progress, mainly in the nature of increasing returns are continuously created and wholly or partially realised."*

Many authorities on the subject believe that industrialisation and agrarian reconstruction in less developing economies are inter-connected and inter-dependent.

Industrialisation has become the watch word of every developing nation. And, so has the study of industrial economics i.e. understanding the management of the industrial sector.

1.2 Meaning and Definitions of Industrial Economics

Industrial Economics is a distinctive branch of economics which deals with the economic problems of firms and industries, and their relationship with society.

There is no clear-cut common agreement on the name of the subject because in economic literature 'industrial economics' is known by several names such as 'Economics of Industries', 'Industry and Trade', 'Commerce', 'Industrial Organisation and Policy' and 'Business Economics' etc.

It was probably through the writings of **P. W. S. Andrews** that the name 'Industrial Economics' was given to the subject. It was in the early fifties. However, even after the popularity of the name 'Industrial Economics', in the American arenas the subject is more popularly known as 'Industrial Organisation'.

The meaning of the term 'Industrial Economics' can be well understood with the following definitions:

1. **J. L. Hanson (Dictionary of Economics and Commerce):** *"Industrial Economics means a term for economic analysis as applied to industry. This branch of applied economics assumed greater importance with the development of business schools."*

2. **Harper Collins (Dictionary of Economics):** *"Industrial Economics is the branch of economics concerned with the functioning of the price system. Industrial economics examines the relationships between market structures, market conduct and market performance using the analytical framework of the theory of markets but within an empirical and dynamic setting".*

3. **Penguin Dictionary of Economics:** *"Industrial Economics is a general term for that branch of applied economics which deals with the factors affecting the structure of industry and the way it is owned and managed. It can, therefore, be regarded as an area of applied micro economics".*

1.3 Nature of Industrial Economics

- Industrial economics studies the various devices of economic management systems and techniques designed to increase efficiency and improve the quality of performance in all the branches and units of industrial production.
- Industrial economics includes the economics of individual branches including power generation, food sectors, coal, oil refining and so on. Each of these sub-divisions of economics examines the economic designation of products, material and technical base, make up of production costs, types of enterprise, differences with respect to fixed capital stock, circulating capital etc.
- Industrial economics is related to several allied fields of knowledge-labour economics, national economic planning, economic geography, technical and mathematical sciences, and so on.

With the above description of the study area of 'industrial economics' the *nature* of the subject can be understood as follows:

1. **An Empirical Discipline:** Industrial economics is predominantly an empirical discipline having micro and macro aspects. It has a strong theoretical base of micro economics and has macro dimensions also.

2. **An Applied Science:** It provides useful applications for industrial management and public policies and has acquired the status of a specialist subject.

3. **An Analyst:** Industrial economics is concerned with the analysis of the markets for which the traditional competitive models are inadequate.

4. **More Realistic:** It is a branch of social science which is interested in what actually happens (positive aspect) rather than what should happen in hypothetical (imaginary) or ideal situations?

5. **Comprehensive Science:** To achieve the broader policy objectives, a state will regulate industries through various ways such as anti-trust policies, nationalisation, control on prices, outputs, credit controls, taxes, etc. A study of all such instruments of industrial regulation is a part of industrial economics. How they influence the performance of the firms is a crucial aspect to be examined under industrial economics. Such information is useful for the regulatory agency of the government to assess the success of its industrial policy.

6. **Empirically Tested:** The conclusions drawn, for example of a firm, may not be testable empirically and therefore we may not be able to assess their predictive efficiency. Industrial economics is free from such limitations as it emphasises on empiricism.

7. **Public Policy:** In 'industrial economics' public policy implications are taken care of, which have been ignored in micro economics. It is true that the theory of firm (micro economics) provides the theoretical base for the study of industrial economics, but several important influences from outside have given a totally different nature to industrial economics.

1.4 Scope of Industrial Economics

The scope of Industrial Economics is very vast. It embraces analytical and descriptive economic analysis as a branch of applied economics.

The areas or fields of its study that indicate the scope of industrial economics are as follows:

1. The subject-matter deals with the basic concept of Industrial Economics.
2. It studies the significance of the theory of studying Industrial Economics.
3. It analyses the inter-relationship between industrial development and economic development.
4. Industrial economics throws light on the factors influencing the location of industries. Under this section, the subject deals with the deductive (**Weber's Theory**) approach of location and inductive (**Sargent Florence's Theory**) approach to the location of industries.
5. It is industrial economics which explains the norms, methods of measuring productivity. Thus, it deals with the factors that determine industrial productivity and what measures should be undertaken to improve productivity.
6. Industrial economics includes the role played by the public sector and private sector with regard to large-scale and small-medium enterprises. It also highlights the problems faced by the industries.
7. Industrial economics explains the profile, development and problems of Special Economic Zones (SEZs).

8. Industrial economics includes within its purview the topic of Industrial Imbalance such as need for having balanced regional development of industries and what are the causes and measures towards industrial imbalance.

9. In its recent development of the subject, it includes the most sought out topic i.e. impact of industrialisation on global warming and on urbanisation.

In short, if Industrial Economics is divided into two elements:

(A) Descriptive Element

It would include the theories of location, meaning of industrial economics, measurement of productivity, industrial profile, meaning of industrial imbalance.

(B) Analytical Element

How does industrial development affect economic development, impact of industrialisation on urbanisation and on global warming, which factors influence location of industrial units, measures to improve industrial productivity etc.

In other words, descriptive element is concerned with the information content of the subject and, the analytical element deals with topics relating to decision-making problems.

1.5 Limitations of Industrial Economics

1. From the time of Adam Smith, Industrial Economics as a study is very *informal and inductive in nature*. This was to develop a meaningful and realistic theory of industrial economics. It was only later when deductive stream of thoughts was developed. However, inductive reasoning was in extensive use.

2. It ignores the idealistic or normative approach. That is it deals with what actually happens rather than what should happen.

3. It is not very comprehensive in nature. In other words, it does not go far in other disciplines for the problem analysis.

4. Adam Smith's 'Wealth of Nations' is a treatise that assumes competitive conditions for the economy in which 'invisible hands' operate to maximise their self-interest. Apart from division of labour, Adam Smith's contribution to the field of industrial economics is the analysis of product pricing. He described two prices, 'natural pricing' and 'market pricing'. Much of his analysis was devoted to determination of 'natural' pricing rather than 'market' pricing.

5. Economists accepted Von Neumann's work on game theory as a break-through in the study of market-structure under conflict. In the context of industrial economics, this theory has many potential uses. However, the full empirical analysis based on game theoretical approach is yet to come.

Despite its few limitations, the subject is rushing fast towards maturity covering both theoretical and empirical dimensions.

1.6 Need and Significance of the Theory of Study of Industrial Economics

As pointed out earlier, there are two broad elements of industrial economics: (A) Descriptive Element and (B) Analytical Element.

(A) Descriptive Element:

The first element of industrial economics is the descriptive element.

1. The descriptive element of industrial economics deals with the *information content of the subject.*

2. It helps to provide the industrialist or businessman with a *survey of the industrial and commercial organisations* of the nation and of other nations with which he may come in contact.

3. The descriptive element of Industrial Economics also gives the *industrialists or businessman the full information* regarding the natural resources, industrial climate in the country, infrastructural situation which would include supplies of factors of production, trade and commercial policies of the governments.

4. It also gives him the degree of *competition in the business* in which he operates.

5. It can be said that "descriptive" element of subject provides *with the information about the competitors, government rules* and *regulations* regarding industry, factors of production and so on.

(B) Analytical Element:

The second element of industrial economics is analytical element i.e. it deals with *business policy and decision-making.*

1. The analytical part deals with topics such as location of plant, investment planning and product diversification, market analysis, pricing policy, choice of techniques, hiring and firing of labour etc. In short, this element of the *subject allows the businessman to analyse the business situation of the nation* and make decisions about investments, diversification, location, technique etc.

2. As it is known that an economic problem arises because of scarcity of means and their alternative uses in relation to the needs of an individual or a group or society as a whole. Similarly, for a producer, the resources like land, raw materials, labour, capital etc. are scarce. Given such scarcity, *he has to take decisions about production and distribution.*

Thus, there are several basic issues on which the producer needs to take decisions-what to produce, level of output, the type of technology to be adopted, scale of his factory, price to be charged and so on. All such decisions explain the producer's *behaviour in the different market situations, which this subject endeavours to study.*

Significance of Industrial Economics:

The subject is rushing fast towards maturity covering both theoretical and empirical dimensions.

1. The evolution of modern industrial economics in the last two hundred years can be traced back to 1776 when the 'Wealth of Nations' of Adam Smith appeared on the scene. This book laid down a strong foundation for the economic theory - the theory of firm - which may be regarded as the mother of the contemporary industrial economics. Since then there has been a steady growth of the field.

2. Apart from division of labour, Adam Smith's contribution to the field of industrial economics is the analysis of product-pricing. His work is regarded as a pioneering study of price-cost margins for industries under competitive conditions.

3. John Robinson's theory of imperfect competition and Chamberlin's analysis of monopolistic competition opened altogether new venues for the industrial economics. Duopoly, oligopoly, product diversification, advertisement behaviour, pricing policy, etc., became burning topics for analysis in industrial economics.

4. **Hotelling** developed the stability conditions for competition by taking differentiated goods and spatial dimensions. Further, his work with Chamberlin's developed altogether a new theory of consumer demand which is very much relevant for industrial economics.

5. Apart from the traditional approach in the framework of market structure, market conduct and market performance link the subject in exploring many interesting new fields of study like strategic behaviour, industrial dynamics, price discrimination, internal organisation, non-price competition, laboratory experiments, financial structure and services, non-cooperative firms, etc.

6. New methods of analysis such as econometrics, game theory, operations analysis, information science, etc., and a substantial rethinking of the causes, nature and effects of competitive behaviour have led to the emergence of New Industrial Organisation having considerable scope for further growth of the subject.

7. Advent of computers and their widespread use in practice have helped considerable growth of empirical work in industrial economics which is expected to increase in future.

Significance of Industrial Economics in relation to Micro Economics:

Some economists believe that industrial economics is just an elaboration and development of the theory of firm under micro economics. In **Stigler's** words, "The field of industrial economics is nothing more than a slightly differentiated micro economics".

However, the *difference between micro economics and industrial economics* would give the need and significance to study industrial economics as a separate distinctive branch of economics.

1. Micro economics is a formal, deductive and abstract discipline, whereas industrial economics is less formal, more inductive in nature.

2. The theory of 'firm' in micro economics focuses on a single goal of the firm- profit-maximisation. Thus, it is passive in approach. On the other hand, industrial economics does not focus only on profit maximisation alone. It concentrates on the constraints which impede the achievement of the goals and tries to remove them, i.e. it is an active discipline.

3. The conclusions derived from micro economics may not be empirically proved and hence its predictions may not be effective. Industrial economics is free from such limitations as the subject emphasises on empiricism (i.e. on tested and tried elements).

4. It is industrial economics that deals with public policy and this subject is ignored in micro economics making industrial economics a more reality in its topics.

5. The theory of 'firm' as dealt in micro economics provides theoretical basis for the study of industrial economics, but several important influences from external sources gives a different character to industrial economics. Thus, it can be said that the traditional theory of firm gets revised in industrial economics.

6. Industrial economics also covers the topics in its scope which are part of managerial economics in business or industrial management such as – concepts and analysis of demand, cost, profit, competition that involve decision-making.

Significance of Industrial Economics in relation to Managerial Economics

The *difference between* the two branches of economics - managerial economics and industrial economics will clarify their respective need to study industrial economics in relation to managerial economics.

1. Managerial economics assumes that the firm aims to maximise its profits and then proceeds to examine the manner in which the firm formulates its rules and procedures to achieve its goal.

    On the other hand, industrial economics differs. In industrial economics the main emphasis is on understanding and explaining the working of the existing economic system and then it predicts the changes that would take place in the 'variables' of the system.

    Thus, 'Industrial Economics' subject matter deals with what actually happens rather than what should happen. This makes Industrial Economics to have a **positive approach** and Managerial Economics to have an **idealistic approach** (or normative approach).

2. It is seen that managerial economics is more inter-disciplinary in nature i.e. accountancy, operations, psychology, research, marketing etc. are integrated with economics in managerial economics (or managerial decision-making).

Industrial economics, on the other hand, is more practical in its problem analysis. It does not go too far in other disciplines for the problem analysis. In fact, the study of industrial economics is the basic element in managerial economics as it provides knowledge of the structural constraints affecting the achievement of the management goals of a firm.

Thus, to achieve the broader policy objectives, a State will regulate industries through ways such as price controls, credit controls, nationalisation, anti-trust policies, taxes etc. And, a study of all such instruments that regulates industries is a part of industrial economics.

These regulations have a great bearing on the performance of the firms and in turn it also guides the government to assess the usefulness of its regulatory agency.

Macro angle significance of Industrial Economics:

- The problem of decision-making in an industry is not only from micro angle, but it has macro dimensions also.
- Not only to an individual industry, but to the society as a whole, the resources for production are scarce. With scarcity of resources arises the problem to produce varieties of goods and services in the present and in future also.
- The problem is to produce 'bread' or 'ammunition'? if 'ammunitions' are preferred, then the series of problems faced by the society may be : what types of ammunitions, in what scale of firm (large, or small); where to produce (problem of location of industry); how to distribute, etc.
- These problems are from individual angle and from the social angle too.
- However, the decisions in context to society as a whole vary from individual producer. Thus, to achieve the broader policy objectives, a state will regulate industries through varieties of ways such as nationalisation, anti-trust policies, credit controls, etc. A study of all such instruments of industrial regulation is very much a part of industrial economics.
- The performance of the firms is a crucial aspect to be examined under industrial economics. And such information is useful for the regulatory agency of the government to access the success of its industrial policy.

To conclude, industrial economics is an empirical discipline enveloping both the micro and macro aspects within itself. Because, like micro economics, it has a strong theoretical base and like macro economics, it provides useful applications for industrial management and public policies.

It has indeed acquired a status of a specialist subject. It can be said that it is not only 'light-throwing' but also 'fruit-bearing' branch of economics.

1.7 Inter-relationship between Industrial Development and Economic Development

Industrial development is a driver of structural change which is key in the process of economic development.

Recent researches suggests that economic development requires structural change from low to high productivity activities and it is the industrial sector that is a key engine of growth in the development process.

The high and sustained economic growth in modern economic development has been associated with industrialisation, particularly growth in manufacturing sector.

"It is only when India has acquired the ability to design, fabricate and erect its own plants without foreign assistance that it will have become a truly advanced and industrialised country". **– Pandit Jawaharlal Nehru**

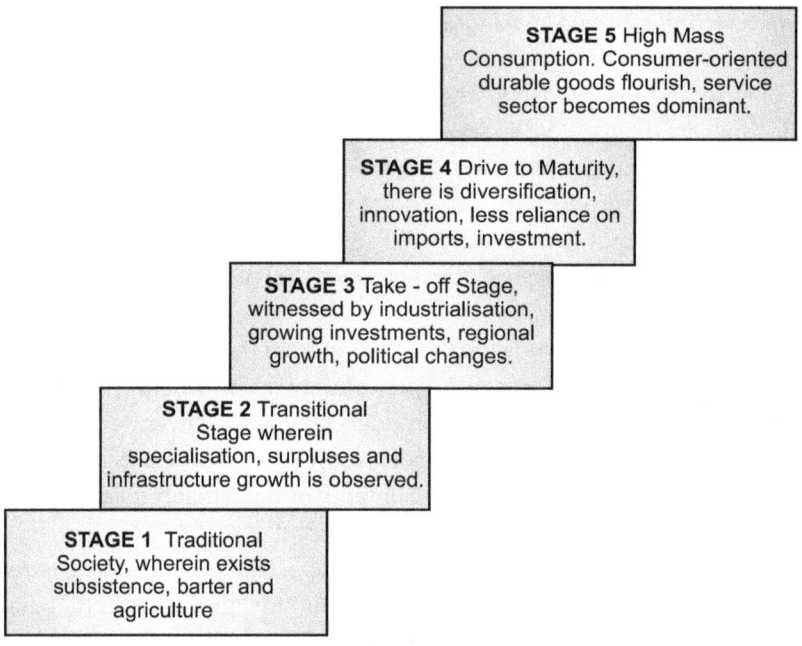

Fig. 1.1: Shows Rostow's Model- the Stages of Economic Development

An essential pre-condition for development is an all-round rise in low productivity occupations to high productivity occupations.

1. It is well-known that the net value of output per person is higher in industry than in agriculture.

2. The scope of internal and external economies is greater in industry than in agriculture.

3. With rapid industrialisation, economies of scale and inter-industrial linkages are predominating.

4. Industrialisation leads to the creation of economic surplus in the hands of industrial producers for further investment.

5. The industrial sector possesses in relation to other sectors, high marginal propensity to save and invest. This in turn contributes to the achievement of a self-sustaining economy which has continuous high levels of investment, high rate of increase in income and industrial employment.

6. Industrialisation process is associated with the development of mechanical knowledge, attitudes and skills of industrial work, industrial management and with other attributes of a modern society. These all elements benefit the growth of productivity in agriculture, trade, distribution and other related sectors of the economy.

7. Due to the improvements in these factors, any successful transfer of labour from agriculture to industry contributes to economic development.

Thus, **industrialisation is inseparable from sustained economic development**, as industrialisation is both a consequence of higher income and a means of higher productivity. **Industrialisation is boosted and so is economic development of the economy with higher income and higher levels of productivity as follows:**

1. When the income levels rise, people have a tendency to spend more on manufactured goods than on basic necessities such as food.

2. The positive income elasticity bestows an advantage on the manufacturing nations in the form of providing expanded market. Higher productivity attracts the labour to manufacturing occupation. This transfer tends to arrest the tendency of diminishing returns in agriculture. Thus, industrialisation acts as an instrument, both of creating capacity to absorb excess labour power (by giving employment) and of catering for the diversification of the market, which is so essential at higher stages of economic development.

3. An urgent requirement for economic development is the diversion of underemployed rural labour to non-agricultural occupations. However, this does not imply that industrial development can be dissociated from progress in agricultural sector :

   (a) In fact, improvement in agricultural productivity creates surplus to be utilised to support increasing labour force in industries.

   (b) It is the agricultural sector supplies that sustain the growing urban population.

   (c) This sector supplies a market for manufactured goods.

   (d) Out of the foreign exchange earnings of agricultural sector, it provides to pay for imported capital goods for industry.

   (e) It provides a source of capital for industry through the medium of capital accumulated by traders and leads to the growth of an exchange economy.

All these factors promote and encourage the growth of manufacturing industry.

Arguments in Favour of Industrialisation related to Economic Development

There are powerful empirical and theoretical arguments in favour of industrialisation as the main engine of growth in economic development.

1. There is an empirical correlation between the degree of industrialisation and per capita income in developing countries.

2. A structural change bonus is to an economy with the transfer of resources from agriculture to manufacturing sector because productivity is higher in the industrial sector than in the agricultural sector.

3. Compared to agriculture, the manufacturing sector offers special opportunities for capital accumulation in developing countries. Capital intensity is high in mining, manufacturing, utilities and transport. It is much lower in agriculture and services. It is true that capital accumulation is one of the aggregate sources of growth; hence an increasing share of manufacturing will contribute to aggregate growth.

4. The manufacturing sector offers special opportunities for economies of scale, which are less available in agriculture or services.

5. Technological advance or progress is concentrated in the manufacturing sector and diffuses from there to other economic sectors such as the service sector.

6. Linkage and spill-over effects are stronger in manufacturing than in agriculture or mining. Linkage effects refer to the direct backward and forward linkages between different sectors. These effects create positive externalities to investments in given sectors. Spill-over effects refer to the externalities of investment in knowledge and technology that flows between sectors.

7. The Engel's law states that as per capita income rise the share of agricultural expenditures in total expenditures declines and the share of expenditures on manufactured goods increases. Thus, nations specialising in agricultural and primary production will not profit from expanding world markets for manufacturing goods.

We have just discussed the inter-relationship between industrialisation and economic development. To be more specific let us discuss in brief as to **why we need industrialisation in India?**

India for long has remained and continues to be predominantly an agricultural country.

(i) Agricultural land in India cannot absorb such vast number of workers in a productive and profitable way. It is said that the marginal productivity of labour in agriculture in India is zero, which means that there is much disguised unemployment in Indian agriculture. It is only the industrial sector that can absorb workers displaced from agriculture. In absence of industrialisation, India will not be in a position to solve the problem of mass unemployment and mass poverty.

(ii) In some cases, the demand for Indian agricultural products is declining as developed industrial nations are opting for synthetic substances like man-made fibres for cotton yarn, plastic wrappings for jute bags etc. This limits the export possibilities in case of products like cotton and jute.

(iii) Even if agriculture is modernised, it would mean displacement of labour by machines and demand for agricultural goods (particularly for food grains) is fairly elastic. Thus, due to low income elasticity of demand for agricultural goods, India cannot increase export quantities of food grains to developed nations.

(iv) Industrialisation is the only answer to India's mass unemployment and poverty. Industries have a large potential to provide productive employment opportunities, due to the operation of the law of increasing returns. In short, industries will provide employment to the masses i.e. masses will earn an income and help alleviate poverty.

(v) In India, value-adding process can be undertaken and enable an increasing number of people earn high level of income. Thus, when industrialisation is there the raw material (instead of exporting) can be utilised in finished goods by India to build a vast network of various industries.

The Agricultural and Industrial Sectors are Integrated with each other

(a) Rapid industrialisation of India implies increasing demand for food grains and other raw material used as 'input' by industries.

(b) Increase in the supply of industrial goods like tractors, electrical and diesel engines will help modernise agriculture and in turn increase per acre and per capita production in the agricultural sector.

(c) Industrialisation not only modernises India's agricultural sector but can provide employment opportunities to the displaced persons from the agricultural sector.

(d) With developed and modernised agriculture and modern industries, India will be less dependent on foreign countries for her vital needs. Thus, modernisation of agriculture and industrialisation will mean more self-reliance. It would reduce our imports and help acquire external equilibrium.

(e) The entire modern defence system is based on the foundation of modern industries. Thus, defence and protection of the country from foreign aggression require that India possesses a strong industrial base.

(f) Industrialisation will introduce new industrial culture-discipline, hard work, team work, self-reliance, inventiveness and organisational ability.

Thus, the inter-relationship between industrialisation and economic development is proved.

Strategy of Industrialisation for Economic Development in Developing Economies:

There is almost universal agreement on the importance of industrialisation, but strategy or pattern of industrial development is equally important.

Historically, industrial development has proceeded in three stages:

(i) Industry concerned with processing of primary goods; e.g. extraction oil, tanning leather, smelting ores etc.

(ii) Second stage comprises the transformation of materials; e.g. footwear, metal goods, furniture etc.

(iii) Third stage consists of manufacture of machines and other capital equipment to facilitate the future process of production.

Hoffmann classified all industrial output into two categories – consumer goods and capital goods output.

Though the general development of industry itself has proceeded from consumer goods to the capital goods, these are variations in the pattern of industrialisation.

In underdeveloped countries the pattern of industrialisation has been guided mainly by considerations arising from scarcity of capital. Thus, the development of labour-intensive consumer goods seems appropriate.

Most of the underdeveloped countries do not produce capital goods at home; the only alternative is to increase their supplies through imports. However, these imports depend upon the rate of growth in exports of primary and manufactured goods. But, due to "export lag" in the exports of primary goods, it does not seem to be a reliable source of foreign exchange earning to increase the import of capital goods.

This does not imply that no developing country has potential to develop. The alternative to increase the exports of primary products is to promote exports of manufacturing goods, i.e. encourage manufacturing industries. There seems to be an obstacle in promotion of export industries, as the advanced countries have a comparative advantage in manufactured goods e.g. in textiles.

Thus, the spread of import-substituting consumer goods industries can release foreign exchange for imports of capital goods.

Import substitution is of two kinds:

(i)   Substitution of home produced goods for imported goods.

(ii) Substitution of capital goods imports for consumer goods imports.

If export-oriented industries are successful in stimulating exports, then it will help increasing the supply of foreign exchange and if import-substitution is effective then the released foreign exchange is identical.

Though, the effect of the development of these two types of industries on foreign exchange is identical, yet import-substituting industry **strengthens the economic independence** of the country. On the other hand, export-oriented industries are subject to fluctuations of price and volume of trade in foreign markets, i.e. it **increases dependence** of the country.

In short, an import-substitution project should be preferred to an export-oriented project.

To conclude,

- Industrial development depends upon the rate of capital formation.
- And, supply of capital can be increased through imports or through domestic production.
- Increased imports depend upon the rate of exports.
- As the scope of exports is limited, export promoting manufacturing industries may be developed or alternatively certain import-substituting domestic industries may be developed.
- This would release foreign exchange for imports of capital goods.
- Alongwith, the current volume of imports, capital goods may be substituted in place of consumer goods.
- Thus, export-promoting industries, import-substituting industries and domestic capital goods industries are complementary to each other.
- *Development of all the three classes of industries, at the same time, will be most effective strategy of industrialisation and to economic development of the country.*

Points to Remember

- Industrialisation has a major role to play in the economic development of the underdeveloped countries.
- Industrialisation has been defined by different economists.
- **Eugene Staley** has linked industrialisation with high productivity.
- Industrial economics is a distinctive branch of economics which deals with the economic problems of firms and industries and their relationship with society.
- Industrial economics – branch of applied economics-assumed greater importance with the development of business schools.

Scope of Industrial Economics:

(i) It studies the significance of the theory of studying Industrial Economics.

(ii) It deals with factors influencing the location of industries.

(iii) It explains the norms and methods of measuring productivity.

(iv) It explains the profile and problems of industries and SEZs.

(v) Industrial Economics is both a descriptive and analytical subject.

Need to Study Industrial Economics:

(i) The descriptive element of industrial economics deals with the information content of the subject. It helps to provide the industrialists with a survey of the industrial and commercial organisation of the nation and other nations with which he may come into contact.

(ii) The analytical element deals with business policy and decision-making.

Inter-relationship between Industrial Development and Economic Development:

- In the beginning of the 19th century industrialisation was closely linked with international trade. It was traditional pattern of growth.
- This 'traditional approach' was out dated when :
  (a) Technological changes led to economic use of new materials.
  (b) Synthetic substitutes.
  (c) Decline in the growth of import demand of the primary products by advanced nations.

Just as, agricultural and industrial sectors are integrated with each other; it implies that industrial development and economic development are integrated and inter-related.

Questions for Discussion

1. State and explain the importance and scope of Industrial Economics.
2. What is Industrial Economics? Explain the need and scope of Industrial Economics.
3. Discuss the inter-relationship between 'Industrial Development and Economic Development'.
4. What is Industrial Economics? Explain in detail the importance and scope of Industrial Economics.
5. Explain the statement, "Industrialisation has a major role to play in the economic development of the underdeveloped countries".
6. Write down the limitations of the study of Industrial Economics.
7. Discuss, in detail, the need and significance of Industrial Economics.

■■■

Chapter **2**...

Theories of Industrial Location

Contents ...

Learning Objectives ...

At the end of the Chapter, you will be able:

- To learn about the meaning of Industrial Location
- To be aware of the factors influencing location of industries
- To understand Alfred Weber's and Sargent Florence's and August Losch's Theories of Location

2.1 Introduction

One of the major problems with which both the management and industry is faced is location i.e. where to locate one's industry. There are various theories which help to understand the meaning of industrial location.

Among the important theories which have been advanced is Weber's theory of Location and Sargent Florence's theory. There are various factors that determine the location of an industry such as availability of raw material, labour, proximity of market, transport, personal factors etc. All these points are covered in detail in the chapter.

2.2 Meaning of Industrial Location

- *"Location of Industries means the methods and desirability of concentrating industries in different areas or localities."* It is with the help of proper location that industrial efficiency becomes possible.

- "Location theory is concerned with the geographic location of economic activity. It has become an integral part of economic geography, regional science, and spatial economics".

- *Location theory deals with questions of what economic activities are located where and why.* Like microeconomic theory it is based on the assumption that firms will choose a location that maximise their profits and individuals choose location that maximise their utility.

- Location of the business is the most significant factor influencing its success or failure. Errors in location may be very difficult and expensive to rectify.

- For any locational plan the major objective is to find out the optimum or best location for the particular plant that would not only result in lowest cost per unit but also facilitate orderly growth of the firm.

- There is no ideal location for all firms or even for one firm at all times as the choice of location depends on several important factors.

- The location of the plant should also be able to meet the environmental guidelines and other regulations set by the Government specific to a particular industry.

  Thus, a manufacturer, while setting up a factory, has to take three inter-related decisions simultaneously;

  1. The scale of operation;
  2. The technique to be adopted which involves the selection of the appropriate combination of the factors of production; and
  3. The location of the production unit.

- All the conventional theories of the firm provides the rules for norms for taking the first two types of decisions i.e. the scale of operation and the technique to be adopted but gives no explanation on the third one i.e. location of the factory. Contributions towards a theory of location of industries made by Classical economists were inadequate except that they made some passing references to the study of location.

- A separate branch of economics bordering with the discipline of geography known as 'Industrial Location' or 'Locational Analysis' deals with the elements of the locational or spatial decision-making.

In this chapter, we will study the theories of industrial location and see how they are operationally useful in deciding the best location for an economic activity. The task of decision-making about industrial location is not very simple. A manufacturer has to consider several technical factors, economic and institutional factors and miscellaneous factors for this. Hence, our first step in this lesson will be to identify such factors.

Problems of Location: The problem of site selection of any factory can be solved in the following three stages:

1. **Selection of the Region:** Generally, the geographical area is divided on the basis of natural regions or political boundaries within the nation e.g. Maharashtra State, Gujarat State etc. The suitability of various regions is considered on the basis of comparative cost advantages available out of the possible regions.

2. **Selection of the Locality:** After selection of the region, the specific locality within the region is considered. For example, urban area, rural area, sub-urban area etc. The suitability of the locality depends on the rules and regulation of the local authorities and the comparative advantage of each locality.

3. **Selection of the Actual Site:** While selecting the actual site, the type of development of land, cost of levelling, possibility of plant expansion and other infrastructural facilities like banking, power, transport, communication etc. are considered.

2.3 Factors Influencing Location of Industries

Development of industries is of utmost importance to an economy. Industrial development is considered to be an index of a country's economic prosperity and strength. The location of industries depends upon a number of geographical, economic and non-economic factors. These factors are known as localisation of industries or agglomeration of industries.

Primarily, industries are governed and guided by the profit motive and the location of an industry can, to a great extent, influence the profitability of any industry. Thus, **maximisation of profit** becomes the major goal in the choice of a particular place for the location of industries. However, there are several factors – technical, economic and institutional – which exert pull and pressure on location of the factory in varying magnitudes.

Factors influencing location of industries can be grouped as:

(A) **Technical Factors:** These are the physical factors and are more or less geographical in nature as they are related to soil, people, climate, raw material etc. These are:

(i)   Availability of land.

(ii)   Nature and quality of raw materials from land. For instance, forest products, minerals, agricultural products (or inputs) and semi-finished goods from existing industries.

(iii)   Climate.

    (iv)   Energy resources.

    (v)   Quantity and quality of human resources.

    (vi)   Availability of waste disposal facilities.

    (vii)   Geographical location of the factory site (or proximity) in relation to the transport facilities like railways, roadways, water and airways.

    (viii)   Water facility for drinking and industrial use.

(B) Economic and Infrastructural Factors: These are :

    (i)   Availability of local markets.

    (ii)   Situation of the export markets.

    (iii)   Costs of land and buildings.

    (iv)   Local cost of living.

    (v)   Taxes and subsidies.

    (vi)   Costs of using infrastructural facilities like transport charges, water-charges, power tariffs etc.

    (vii)   Wages in relation to skills.

    (viii)   Availability and cost of finance.

    (ix)   Housing facilities.

    (x)   Local medical facilities.

    (xi)   Industrial relations and trade union activities around the proposed location sites.

    (xii)   Communication facilities.

    (xiii)   Cultural facilities like schools, clubs etc.

    (xiv)   Demographic factors such as population, sex-ratio, and literacy rate etc.

(C) Miscellaneous Factors: Other factors can be divided into two categories:

    1.   Government policies towards location of new plants, and

    2.   Personal factors.

As for Government policies, most of the governments pursue the policy of rapid industrialisation of their states. They provide several facilities for locating new plants in some regions or places. An entrepreneur has to examine the facilities provided by the Government very carefully before taking a decision on location of his factory.

In case of *personal factors* determining the location of industries it can be said that:

    (a) a manufacturer may prefer to locate his factory at his birth place disregarding all economic factors;

    (b) he may set up his factory close to any recreational centre.

In short, industrial location based on such personal factors will entirely be a matter of chance or what is called as 'historical accident'. Examples of personal factors influencing location of industries are automobile factories of Ford at Detroit and of Morris at Oxford.

Let us discuss some of the 'general' factors in detail:

1. Availability of Raw Materials: In determining the location of an industry, nearness to raw material availability and assurance of regular supply of cheap raw material is of utmost significance.

For most major industries, the cost of raw materials forms the bulk of the total cost. Nearness to the sources of raw materials would reduce the cost of production of the industry. Hence, most of the agro-based and forest-based industries and mineral-based industries are located in the vicinity of the sources of raw material supply.

The pull towards the sources of raw materials would be greater in the case of industries requiring localised gross materials. That is, industries are set up close to or in the regions where raw material is available in plenty. This leads to localisation of jute industry in West Bengal, Sugar industry in Uttar Pradesh.

If the raw material is heavy and of small value, the industries are set up in the regions of raw material, for example, Iron smelting, brick making, cement manufacturing.

Where several materials (weight-losing and bulky) are combined into a single commodity, such industries are near the source of raw material. For example, the Iron and Steel Industry requires several raw materials such as iron ore, coal, lime-stone etc. which is bulky and weight-losing materials, hence iron and steel industry has a tendency to be 'raw-material-localised'. For example, Iron and Steel Plants have been set up in proximity to the sources of raw material such as at Bhilai (Chhattisgarh), Rourkela (Orissa), Durgapur (West Bengal), and Jamshedpur (Jharkhand).

In other words, most of the agro-based, forest-based and mineral-based industries are to be located in the proximity to the source of raw material supply.

2. Labour: The availability of cheap labour, skilled and unskilled in a region is an important factor determining the localisation of industries. The attraction of an industry towards labour centres depends on the ratio of labour cost to the total cost of production which **Weber** calls 'Labour Cost of Index'.

The availability of skilled workers in the interior parts of Bombay region was one of the factors responsible for the initial concentration of cotton textile industry in the region. The development of the plantations in Assam is attributed to the availability of cheap efficient labour.

Different types of industries require different types of labour force. For example, watch-making, electronics, computer industries etc., require highly skilled labour, whereas sugar making, jute textile etc., employ more of unskilled labour.

3. Nearness to Markets: Market is an important factor determining localisation of industries:

    (i)   Those that produce bulky, heavy goods that are expensive to transport;

    (ii) Those that produce perishable or fragile goods;

    (iii) Those that provide services to people.

Industries producing perishable commodities which cannot be transported over a long distance and/or industries that produce bulky goods, involving heavy transportation costs are located in close proximity to markets, examples' in the case of bread and bakery, ice, etc. Industry should be located near the markets and could reduce the costs of transport in distributing the finished product.

Further, accessibility of markets is more important in the case of industries manufacturing consumer goods rather than producer goods as they need adjustments constantly with the changes in the habits of the consumers.

For example, paper mill industry which is concentrated at Kolkata and Raniganj, they have a command over large markets in and around Kolkata. Most of the mills in Kolkata manufacture stationery and printing paper for which there is a ready market on hand. This example depicts concentration of the industry near to the market. However, in the dispersal of industrial activity, evolution of new markets is an important factor.

The market is not so important for other industries such as high-tech whose products are light in weight and cheap to transport. Such industries are said to be 'footloose'.

4. Transport Facilities: A good transport network helps reduce costs and make the movement of materials easier. Industries depend upon efficient and cheap transportation system, which is essential for the movement of raw material as well as the finished products.

The transportation with its three modes, i.e., water, road and rail collectively plays an important role. So, the junction points of waterways, roadways and railways become humming centres of industrial activity as they can enjoy benefits of easy transportation from different directions.

Besides the modes, the rates of transport and transport policy of Government considerably influence the location of industrial units. For example, in the location of cement industry, transport relations of a centre in regard to raw materials, markets and power are the dominating factors.

Thus, cement industry has a tendency to be attracted at the point of minimum transport costs in relation to raw material markets and power. Even in the case of Iron and Steel Industry, especially, in the Visakhapatnam steel plant, transport plays an important role. Even the heavy concentration of cotton textile industry in Mumbai has been due to the cheap and excellent transportation network both in regard to raw materials and markets.

5. Power: Another factor influencing the location of an industry is the availability of cheap power. Water, wind, coal, gas, oil and electricity are the chief sources of power. Thus, the sources of energy have a vital decisive influence in the location of industrial units because an industry needs cheap power.

In the initial days of industrial evolution, industrial units used to depend upon coal and coal being bulky and weight-losing material, during the 19th century, nearness to coal fields became the principal locating influence on the setting up of new industries, particularly for heavy industries. But with the introduction of other sources of power, the power factors in location of industries became more flexible. The pattern of location distribution of most of the industries has considerably changed with the development of hydro-electricity. It can be said that electric power is helping in the dispersal and decentralisation of most of the industries, even if not all.

6. Site and Services: Existence of public utility services, cheapness of the value of the site, amenities attached to a particular site like the level of ground, the nature of vegetation and location of allied activities influence the location of an industry to a certain extent.

'Industrial Estates' scheme has been launched by the Government of India to accelerate and to help dispersal of industrial activity over a wider area in the country. To develop the backward regions, entrepreneurs are granted various incentives like subsidies or are provided finance at concessional interest, supply power at cheaper tariffs, provided education and training facilities, when they set up industrial unit in these classified backward areas. Some entrepreneurs induced by such incentives may come forward to locate their units in such areas.

7. Finance: Development of industries requires a large capital investment. It may come from any source, local or foreign. Banks and other financial institutions play a significant role in the growth of industries.

The availability of capital at cheap rate of interests and in adequate amounts is a determining factor in industrial location. For example, in case of jute industry, besides availability of raw materials and transport facilities, the capital provided by the Scottish enterprise played a dominating role in the establishment of new units and in the expansion of existing units in and around Kolkata.

Another example, a review of 'location' history of Indian cotton textile industry indicates that concentration of the industry in and around Bombay in the early days was chiefly due to the presence of rich and enterprising Parsi and Bhatia merchants, who supplied vast financial resources.

Due to the mobility of the capital, it can be raised nationally and internationally. Hence, in location of industrial units, financial considerations are not likely to exert much influence.

8. Natural and Climatic Factors: Level of ground, topography of a region, water facilities, disposal of waste products, drainage facilities etc., influence the location of industries. For instance, the humid climate of Mumbai in India and Manchester in Britain offered great scope for the development of cotton textile industry in those centres. Again, in the manufacturing process certain industries require an adequate and steady supply of water. In such a case such industries may be influenced by this factor.

9. Personal Factors: When deciding location of industrial unit, at times an entrepreneur may have personal preferences and prejudices against certain localities. Examples can be cited of Ford, automobile industry in Detroit was started as it was his home town. Lord Nuffield selected Crowley, because the school in which his father was educated happened to be for sale. In above examples, we find that in determining industrial location, personal factor dominates other considerations.

At times, personal whims, prejudices of an entrepreneur matter in setting up of an industry in an area, ignoring all the economic and commercial considerations.

In a democratic set up, sometimes political matters initiate the set-up of certain heavy industries in certain regions. For example, the setting up of a Railway Coach Factory at Kapurthala in Punjab was set up due to political interest rather than economic considerations.

10. Strategic Factors: In modern times, strategic factors play a vital role in determining location of an industrial unit. For example, during war-time a safe location is assuming special importance. The reason is that during the war the main targets of air attacks would be armaments and ammunition factories and industries supplying other goods which are required for war. The Russian experience during the Second World War supports this factor for localisation of industries.

11. External Advantages: External economies (or economic benefits) exert considerable influence on the location of industries. External economies arise due to the growth of specialised subsidiary activities when a particular industry is mainly localised at a particular centre. External economies are also enjoyed when a large number of industrial units in the same industry were located in close proximity to one another.

12. Government Policy: To encourage industries in the country, the government provides certain guidelines, tax holidays, electricity at concessional rates, subsidies, etc. Government policy plays a significant role in determining location of an industry. For example, if the government bans import of foreign cars, the automobile industry is bound to flourish in that country.

13. Other Factors: Historical accidents play a dominating role in determining the location of industries. The cotton industry first settled in Lancashire for no particular reason except, perhaps, that the woollen industry was already there and that foreigners were kindly received and Manchester was not a Corporation.

The size of an industrial unit influences the location because the size of industrial unit depends upon the radius of the circle within which they can profitably distribute their commodities and upon the density of population living within the circle.

Climate also plays an important part in the location of industries. The stimulating cool temperate climate is suitable for the development of industries as this type of climate add to the work efficiency of the labour force. For example, temperate latitudes have well-developed manufacturing industries rather than the desert or the Tundra regions.

Thus, these are a few major location factors assuming all other factors either constant or irrelevant. This is quite natural as a comprehensive location model which incorporates all the factors is difficult to construct.

Dynamics of Industrial Location

In order to understand the precise relevance of the various location factors and the interactions among themselves, let us examine the leading approaches to industrial location analysis.

There are various factors which influence location of an industry, but none of these factors can continue to have its effectiveness for all times to come. A factor which might be very important today, might become less tomorrow or might even lose its usefulness altogether. Thus, changes in different location factors can bring a shift in the location of an industrial activity. Though every state desires to have locational equilibrium in industrial development yet, many a times locational changes do occur. **E. M. Hoover** has classified basic causes of locational changes as follows:

1. **Seasonal Changes:** Sometimes, producers shift their location so as to meet changing seasonal needs and requirements. But the producer knows that in a particular season he will have to shift and as such he is quite prepared for that and can change location without much dislocation. Thus, he is not taken unaware. For example, in California beekeeping is seasonally migratory. Thus, he knows the seas and nature of his industry.

2. **Cyclical Changes:** These changes occur due to fluctuations in business cycle. Such changes are not as predictable and regular as seasonal changes in the location of actual production occur at all stages of the business cycle.

3. **Secular Changes:** A secular change is one which is not sudden but which involves a gradual growth of a change. Such a change continues for quite some time. It has no tendency to reverse or repeat itself as in case of seasonal and cyclical changes. For example, growth in population that can bring changes in demand and can influence the location of an industry.

4. **Structural Changes:** Development of new resources and techniques can bring about changes in location of industry. Every major technological improvement is likely to bring about locational change. In the words of **Prof. S. C. Kuchhal**, "Modern technical innovations have made labour requirements less specialised and exacting.

They also have involved decentralisation to new centres of production. Further the vastly increased use of non-human industry in production has been offset by improved techniques that make energy cheaper and more transmissible and tend to equalise the advantage of various locations in respect of energy cost".

Localisation of industry has its own advantages and disadvantages which may be briefly summed up as under:

Advantages of Localisation:

- One of a major advantage of localisation is that the product gets reputation and demand for that product by the consumer is created without much sales propaganda.
- Another advantage when the industry is localised is that specialised labour develops and gets much encouragement. In this way, considerable industrial skill is preserved.
- In that area means of transportation and communication develop and these become available to the society easily and at cheap rates.
- The financers also easily assist the localised industries. Other facilities such as training of the workers, conducting research can be easily and economically arranged when big industrial units are localised and naturally the subsidiary industries are also centralised there. These ancillaries or dependent industries flourish and grow together with big industries. Last but not the least advantage of localisation is that organisation of workers as well as those of the industrialists becomes very easy and convenient.

Disadvantages of Localisation:

Localisation of industries also suffers from certain demerits.

- During war days enemy can make localised industrial complex as target of attack and destruction. This gives a serious setback to the nation. This is the reason why strategic factors are getting preference over economic factors.
- Another disadvantage is that special skill labour gets concentrated at one place and mobility of labour receives a setback which is not beneficial to the society as a whole.
- With increased localisation problems of housing, high rents, unhygienic conditions, over-crowding etc. are commonly witnessed.
- Localisation of industries gives rise to unfavourable conditions like local strikes, outbreak of fire etc. The conditions are worsened during depression. Economic dependence on the area increases which is undesirable on the part of the nation.

Economic Survey of Site Selection:

The necessary factors in the selection of plant location vary from industry to industry and with changing technical and economic conditions. Therefore, a location survey must be carried out based on the specific requirements of a given enterprise.

The aim of such economic survey is to find out whether or not the location meets the primary and secondary requirements (i.e. factors influencing the location of industries). It is true that the relative importance of the necessary factors can be determined on the basis of their proportionate share in the unit cost of production and distribution. After the various factors have been weighed, suitable site can be selected.

Selection of Actual Site: The important factors in this respect are:

1. Availability of cheap land to set-up and for expansion of the plant.
2. Cost of land development. The land should be flat and strong enough to sustain heavy machine installation. For agro-based industries the type of soil should be considered.
3. Facilities for upkeep and general maintenance should be available in nearby areas.
4. Facilities for housing the workers and if necessary their transport from the place of residence to the work site.
5. Social and recreational facilities.
6. Post and telegraph facilities.
7. Cost of laying the water supply and provision of sewage and disposal of waste.
8. Cheap facilities for disposal of trade waste.
9. Any restrictions imposed by the town planning department, local bye-laws etc.
10. Taxes, fire protection facilities etc.

Computation of Investment and Cost of Production of Distribution:

The required capital investment and the unit cost of production and distribution for a given volume of output should be computed for each prospective location.

- An ideal location is one which permits the lowest cost of production and its distribution.
- If the unit costs of the production in the various locations are somewhat comparable, the location that requires the least capital or fixed investment will be preferred.
- The choice should be checked against detailed information obtained from local banks and Government agencies.

Selection of the Site: Urban, Rural and Suburban area. There are broadly three possible alternatives open for the selection of the locality of the industrial unit.

(i) Urban or city area;

(ii) Rural area;

(iii) Suburban area

The relative advantages and disadvantages of each area determine the selection of a site for an industrial unit.

Recent Trends in the Location of Industries:

The traditional factors like nearness of source of raw materials, nearness of market, labour supply, motive power etc. have no longer remained the effective pulling forces in the location of industries. The locational trends have changed substantially due to the development of substitute raw materials, network of electrification and transportation by road and railways, mobility of labour and with persuasive and compulsive policies of the government for the balanced regional development.

Thus, the recent trends in the selection of industrial location can be attributed to following changes:

(a) **Priority for Suburban Areas:** The industrialists show their preference for the suburban area as the site for establishment of a new unit or for relocation of the existing one. The Industrial Policy of the government does not permit the establishment of new unit or expansion of existing unit in city areas. At the same time infrastructural facilities are developed in the suburban areas.

(b) **Industrial Development in the Notified Backward Areas:** In order to have balanced regional development, the Central Government as well as the State Government has notified certain backward areas, for example, Baruch, Surendranagar, Panchamahals are centrally notified backward districts of Gujarat State. Different types of incentives like cash subsidy, tax reliefs, concessional financial assistance, cheaper land etc. are provided. So, many such areas have attracted industrialists to set-up their unit in recent times.

(c) **Establishment of Industrial Estates:** The Government of India assigned the responsibility of the development of industrial estates to State Governments. The plots of the land alongwith factor shades and infrastructural facilities are developed in the industrial estates and are sold to the prospective promoters. The establishment of industrial estates have greatly affected the location of industries.

(d) **Decentralisation of Industries:** Under the conscious Industrial Policy of the government, concentration of industrial units is prevented through licensing policy. New units are not given permission in certain industrially congested areas. Similarly, existing units either establish their additional plant in less developed area or relocate the whole unit in such areas.

(e) **Increased Role of the Government in the Decision of Location of Industries:** The government through its persuasive and compulsive methods greatly influence the location of an industrial unit in recent times. It provides certain attractive incentives to the promoters to establish their units in less developed areas and at the same time does not permit excessive industrialisation in certain developed areas through taxes and penalties or other restrictions.

(f) Competition between Government and Institutions: As industry provides job opportunities to the local population, many local authorities attract the prospective promoters to establish the units in their areas. They provide different types of incentives such as relief in local taxes, cheap land etc. At times, the objective of local authorities and the government comes in conflict on the issue of location of industries.

Thus, the whole pattern of decision about the location of industries has undergone substantial change in the recent times.

Government Control on Location of Industries:

The main motive of private sector is profit maximisation. As such, entrepreneurs select such a site which reaps maximum economic advantage. Such an attitude results into the localisation or concentration of industries in certain areas leaving other areas underdeveloped. It distorts the principle of equality of income, wealth and opportunity in the economy. Thus, the government being the custodian of public interest intervenes in the locational decisions of the industrial units as under:

(i)   Through the licensing policy, it restricts the concentration of industries in developed areas.

(ii) Provides attracting incentives for spread of industries in the industrially backward areas.

(iii) It establishes giant public sector units in the relatively less developed areas and thus encourages growth of ancillary units around it.

The Objectives of State Intervention are:

(i)   To attain balanced regional development.

(ii) To narrow down the gap of inequalities of income and wealth by creating and providing employment opportunities to less developed areas.

(iii) To reduce the concentration of population and congestion of industries in city areas.

(iv) As strategic defence policy, spread of industries reduces the chances of heavy losses during war time.

2.4 Theories of Industrial Location

Introduction

*   The location of the plant has great influence on the production system. The plant location has direct influence on the costs of production operations as well as on the marketing efficiency; and once a location is finalised, the industrialists is forced to remain in that location for many years. Hence, any error in deciding the plant location leads to long-term problems. Thus, an industrialist has to be very careful while deciding the plant location.

- An entrepreneur should anticipate the future requirements of his enterprise to make long-range forecasts before he finalises the location of his unit. Such forecasts should be based on the expansion policy of the unit, the anticipated diversification of products, the changing market trends, the sources of raw materials and other influences. An entrepreneur should also analyse the current relationship of the factors affecting the location of the plant.

- The main aim of every industrial unit is to maximise profits through the minimisation of cost of production. This can be achieved only when the firm, apart from being the optimum size, is located at a place which provides internal and external economies in production. In other words, the unit has to be a combination of optimum size at optimum location.

The different theories of industrial location can be explained as under:

Traditional Approach to the problem of Location:

Classical economists like **Adam Smith, J. S. Mill, and Alfred Marshall** were of the opinion that location decisions were always based on factors like personal choice due to local loyalty of the entrepreneur, availability of raw materials, market and traditionally skilled labour. Lack of mobility of these factors due to undeveloped transport system, elementary mechanism and consequent dependence on skilled workers were coming in the way of an ideal location without requiring analysis relating to the place where the predominant factor was prevailing. These economists analysed the various factors of location based on empirical analysis rather than on a scientific treatment of the problem. In fact, they did not evolve any satisfactory theory of location.

2.4.1 Alfred Weber's Theory of Industrial Location

Alfred Weber, a German economist, has developed one of the earliest approaches to explain the location of manufacturing industry.

Earlier to Weber, another German economist **Launhardt** has given a simple principle of industrial location based on **minimum transport cost.**

However, Weber's work in this field may be regarded as the starting point of modern systematic study and theorisation of the subject of industrial location.

Weber's theory of location is purely **deductive** in its approach. Hence Weber's interest was to construct a **general theory of location** which could be applied to all industries at all times. For this, he has taken into account the general factors of location which were relevant to all industries.

The influencing factors considered by Weber were divided into two groups:

(A) Those influencing inter-regional location of industries (i.e. regional factors);

(B) Those influencing intra-regional location (i.e. agglomerating factors).

The *regional* factors were:

(i)　Raw material costs;

(ii)　Transport cost; and

(iii) Labour cost.

Friedrich observed that fluctuations in raw material costs (point i) were included within transport costs (point ii).

Thus, the approach of location analysis followed by **Weber** was to explain industrial location in terms of transport cost (point ii) first and then to examine the effects of changes in labour cost (point iii) and then the factors influencing intra-regional location, i.e., agglomerative factors on it.

Assumptions: The underlying assumptions for his analysis are as follows:

1.　The location of raw materials including fuel is fixed.

2.　The situation and size of consuming centres are given.

3.　There are several fixed labour centres; labour is immobile and unlimited in supply at fixed wage rate.

4.　Weber also assumed the institutional factors like taxation, interest, insurance etc. As insignificant location factors.

5.　The economic, culture and political system are treated to be uniform and stable across the locations.

On the whole, Weber assumed *perfect competition for his model.*

According to Weber, only two basic factors are left for consideration in determining the location of an industry:

(i)　Transport cost; and

(ii)　Labour cost.

An industrial unit must incur transport costs in respect of raw materials; fuel etc., since they are not available at the same place.

The industrial unit, thus, has to choose such a location that minimum are its total transportation cost.

The key factors that determine transportation costs are:

(i)　The weight to be transported, and

(ii)　The distance to be covered.

By no means will all the deposits (raw materials etc.) necessarily be located near to the place of consumption. In such a case, the optimal position will be chosen, where the location of an industry will be determined in relationship to the place of consumption and to the most advantageously located material deposits.

For this the 'location figures' are created. (Transportation Costs).

The 'location figure' depends upon (a) the type of material deposits, and (b) the nature of transformation into products.

- Raw materials which are practically everywhere are called as **'Ubiquities'** e.g. brick-clay, water etc.
- And, raw materials that are available only in certain regions are called as **'localised'** e.g. iron-ore, minerals, wood etc.
- It can be thus clearly understood that *localised materials play an important role on the industry than the ubiquities.*

Further, Weber classifies raw materials as 'pure' and 'weight-losing' as regards the nature of the transformation of materials into products.

- 'Pure' materials are those which impart their total weight to the products e.g. cotton, wool etc.
- And, the materials are referred to as 'weight-losing' if only a part enters into the product e.g. wood, coal etc.
- Needless to say that the location of industries using **weight-losing** materials is drawn towards their **deposits** and that of industries using **'pure' materials** towards the **consumption centres** (or markets).

Weber used the 'location triangle' of **Launhardt** to find the place of minimum transport cost.

A simple spatial situation is assumed in which only one consumption centre (C) and two fixed supply centres – M_1 and M_2 for two important raw materials.

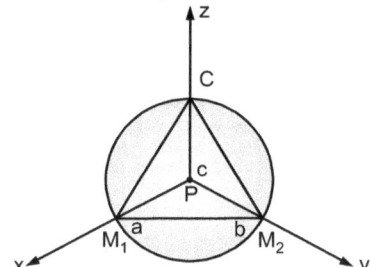

Fig. 2.1: Weber's Theory of Industrial Location

According to **Weber**, the least cost point will be located within the triangle $CM_1 M_2$ such as the one shown by P.

The three corner points of the triangle will be pulling the location point P towards themselves. The position of P will depend on the balance of pulls exercised by them. If the pull of any one corner is more than the aggregate pulls of other corners, then production will be located at the point of origin of the dominant forced. The force exerted by each corner on production point is in the form of ton-mile weight to be moved from the point M_1 and M_2 and to the point C i.e. from the supply centres of raw materials M_1 and M_2) to the consumption centre (C) as a finished product.

Let x and y be the requirements of materials, M_1 and M_2 in tons per ton of output and let one unit of output i.e. finished product to be transported from point P to C.

The distances of the corner points from the production point P are unknown. Let them be a, b and c between P and M_1, M_2 and C points respectively. Thus, the total ton-miles of transport per unit of output would be ax + by + c. This is to be minimised to find the location of production i.e. position of point P. The distances a, b and c and hence point P are easy to be found by applying the theorem of parallelogram of forces in geometry.

Based on simple deductions, Weber has formulated the 'laws of transportation'. **Weber is of the view that governing factor on location of industry is the extent to which localised materials impart their weight to the final product.**

The proportion of the weight of localised material to the weight of the product is known as 'material index' of an industry.

The material index (MI) is defined as:

MI = (Weight of localised material) ÷ (Weight of finished product)

Weber used the 'material index' for identifying whether an industry may be material-oriented or market-oriented.

- All industries whose material index is greater than one (MI > 1) are attracted towards the sources of raw materials such as iron and steel industry.
- When industries have material index less than one (MI < 1) and whose 'location weight' is not greater than two lie at the place of consumption.
- 'Pure materials' can never bind production to their deposits.

Deviation in location of industry (Labour Costs)

Weber also examines the reason as to why an industrial unit will *deviate* from the centre of least transport costs.

It is the differences in *labour costs* that lead an industry to deviate from the optimal point of transport.

Such migration of an industry from a point of minimum transport costs to a cheaper labour centre may be likely to occur only where the *savings in the cost of labour are larger than the additional costs of transport* which it ought to incur.

Weber used the average cost of labour per unit weight of product as an index. Greater the labour cost index more will be the industry's deviation from **the least transport cost site**.

Weber suggested using the industry's 'co-efficient of labour'. This is defined as the labour cost per ton of location weight, where:

Location Weight = Weight of material and product ÷ Weight of product.

= Material Index (MI) + 1

A high 'co-efficient of labour' means a strong attraction to the cheap labour location.

E. A. G. Robinson, in his work on the "Structure of Competitive Industry" concludes the **Weber's** techniques with regard to the factors which determine the location of production into two broad groups:

1. The factors which determine where the **transport costs involved will be at a minimum**.
2. The factors which make **for lower costs of production** at some places than at other places.

Agglomerative Factors: (Factors influencing intra-regional location).

The next important step in Weber's theory is to examine the effects of agglomeration.

An agglomerative factor is an 'advantage' or cheapening of production or marketing which results from the fact that production is carried on to some considerable extent *at one place*.

Thus, agglomeration means *concentration of production for a commodity at one place that result in economies of scale within a plant and economies from the association of several plants*.

Economies of association is realised from specialised division of labour between plants, better repair facilities, a specialised labour market, lowering of social overhead costs.

A deglomerative factor is a cheapening of production which results from the decentralisation of production i.e. carrying on production in *more than one place*.

To a certain extent these agglomerative and deglomerative factors also contribute to local accumulation or distribution of any industrial unit.

However, these factors will operate only within the general framework formed by the two regional factors i.e. costs of transportation and costs of labour. Weber treats, these factors to have influence over the deviation of the location of industry from the minimum transport point. For instance, the agglomerative factors such as gas, water-mains etc. tends to the concentration of industry and the deglomerative factors which follows from the rise in the land value, taxes etc. lead to decentralisation.

Agglomerative factors that attract an industrial unit to a particular point operate through two factors:

(i)   It depends on the 'index of manufacture' (i.e. the proportion of manufacturing costs to the total weight of the product).

(ii) It depends on the 'location weight' (i.e. the total weight to be transported during all the stages of production).

To arrive at a general principle, Weber uses the concept of "co-efficient of manufacture". "Co-efficient of manufacture" **is the ratio of manufacturing cost to location weight**. When the co-efficient of manufacture is high, then agglomeration is encouraged (i.e. concentration of production) and deglomeration is when it is low co-efficient of manufacture.

It is to be understood that labour orientation is one form of deviation from the minimum point and agglomeration is another factor. Now, when agglomerative factors appear in an industry (economies appear) that is labour-oriented, there takes place a competition between the agglomerative deviation and the labour deviation then one of the two forces which can offer the greater net economies over and above the transport orientation will be the winner.

Critical Evaluation:

Weber's analysis of industrial location is indeed a pioneering one. It has paved the way for development of programming models for industrial location. Although **Alfred Weber's** original contribution on the theory of location provoked thinking and stimulated a great deal of research. Yet, a concrete explanation could not be provided for the location of industry in all its aspects. **Weber's** techniques were severely criticised by **A. Robinson, Sargant Florence, S. R. Dennison, Andreas Predohl** on various grounds:

1. **Unrealistic approach:** Weber's techniques has been criticised for his unrealistic approach and deductive reasoning. According to Sargant Florence, vague generalisations cannot provide suitable solutions to the theory of location as non-economic considerations will also influence which are not mentioned in the pure theory. He says that Weber's theory fails to explain locations resulting from historical and social forces.

2. **Division of raw materials:** A. Robinson raises objections to Weber's method of analysis. The division of raw materials into 'ubiquities' and 'localised' is considered artificial. Robinson agreed that on certain essential differences in the character of the commodities, this classification might have been done and it was relevant for enumerating a location theory.

3. **An unrealistic assumption:** Weber assumes labour orientation, that is, fixed labour centres and secondly, unlimited supplies of labour has been assumed. However, it has been criticise that the rise of industry may create new labour centres and we cannot assume unlimited labour supplies at any centre.

4. **Selective theory:** Andreas Predohl criticises Weber's theory as more a selective than deductive theory while referring to the Weber's classification of regional factors (primary factors) and agglomerative factors (secondary factors) that influence location trend. This distinction is artificial, illogical and arbitrary.

5. **Non-monetary terms: S. R. Dennison** points out that the approach towards the theory of location as presented by Weber is overburdened with technical considerations. His theory stresses in terms of technical co-efficient and is devoid of all cost and price factors. Dennison remarks that Weber's theory instead of measuring

the saving in labour costs (labour-oriented unit) in terms of ton-miles; it should have been measured in money terms, which is more natural and real in any economic analysis.

6. **Fixed consumption points is unrealistic:** In a competitive market structure, the assumption of fixed points of consumption is quite unrealistic. The country wise scattering of consuming public is usually a reality and in fact there may be a shift in the consuming centres with a shift in industrial population.

In spite of the shortcomings, Weber's deductive theory is the only theory which has been enjoying the universal acceptance and application, as all other alternative suggestions are not comprehensive in nature.

Modifications:

Weber's deductive theory of location needs some modifications as to make it more practical in application.

1. Dennison contends that Weber's theory is particularly in terms of technical co-efficient. This can be eliminated to a great degree, if calculations are introduced in terms of costs and prices, wherever practicable.

2. The assumption of fixed consumption centres needs to be revised. This assumption should receive lesser importance as labour is mobile. Further, Weber's theory assumes availability of unlimited supplies of labour. This unconvincing assumption should be given-up. Existence of unstable wage levels in the labour centres should be taken into consideration.

3. In the assumption of transportation costs, only distance to be covered and weight to be transported is considered. In real, the actual rate schedules must be consulted relating to different transport media to make the concept of transport orientation more appropriate. And, if there is any saving in transportation due to substitution, it should be expressed in terms of actual costs and not in ton-miles.

Andreas Predohl's Approach:

Andreas Predhol argued that every change of location of industries involves a change in the combination in the means of production. Predohl felt that the problem of relocating the plant of shifting it from one place to another was just a variation of the general theory of substitution. Thus, according to him if an industry shifts from a particular place – for e.g. from Mumbai to Pune – he is of the view that it will be because of certain added advantages at the new location – Pune. But this approach cannot explain the factors determining the location of an altogether new industry.

2.4.2 Sargent Florence's Theory of Location

Prof. Sargent Florence's theory of location has assumed great practical importance and has acquired a wide popularity in the recent years.

Prof. Florence felt that Weber's theory of location was based on many unrealistic assumptions. He was very critical about Weber's geographical aspect of location. *He believed that more important the relation of an industry to an area was the relation of the industry to the distribution of the occupied population as a whole.*

Hence, he does not accept the meaning of localisation i.e. relation of an industry to geographical area. He gave greater importance to the relation of the industry to the distribution of the occupied population.

For this he takes the occupational distribution of the population.

In working out the statistical measures of the degree of location of different industries, he relied on the census of production.

As against Weber's deductive theory, Florence's is mainly an inductive analysis. He makes use of two new concepts 'location factor' and 'co-efficient of localisation' to explain the existing location pattern of an industry.

(A) 'Location Factor': It implies an index of the **degree of concentration** of an industry in **a particular region**. This index is measured by taking two ratios:

   (a) The percentage of workers of the industry in question found in the region under consideration, and

   (b) The percentage of all industrial workers found in that particular region to the total industrial workers in the country.

The first one is to be divided by the second one to find out the location factor.

The location factor is said to **be unity** (even distribution of industry in the whole country) when the quotient **is one.**

If the location factor is **greater than unity**, that region **has high concentration of the industry**. If the location factor is **less than unity**, that region does not have a sufficient share of the industry.

'Location factor' is calculated for the regions, based on the political divisions of a country and not into industrial zones, as it is possible, though not very scientific.

(B) 'Co-efficient of Localisation': It shows the propensity of an industry for concentration, i.e. it is the tendency of attraction or repulsion exercised by the existence of units or unit of an industry in a region for other units of the industry.

This co-efficient of localisation refers **to a particular industry and not to a particular region**. Further, it may be in relation to an industry's' tendency for localisation anywhere in the nation. It means that even when location factor would be different from area to area, but the 'co-efficient of localisation' would be a single figure for the industry and for the country as a whole.

Co-efficient of localisation is measured as:
(i)   The percentage of all workers found in each region is to be calculated.
(ii)   The percentage of the workers of the industry in question in each region is to be calculated.
(iii) The positive deviations of (ii) from (i) are to be summed up.
(iv)   The sum derived is to be divided by 100.
The result, now obtained, will be co-efficient of localisation.

With the co-efficient of localisation, all industries of a country can be put into three categories – high, medium and low co-efficient industries.

Industries with high co-efficient show very little tendency of dispersal (i.e. there is high concentration) e.g. industrial units localised near the source of raw material. And, industries with low co-efficient can thrive in any region i.e. they show greater propensity to disperse.

Thus, the main objective of finding the concept of co-efficient of localisation is to classify industries according to their qualities of dispersion or concentration.

Critical Evaluation:
1. The theory could not be considered as an independent flawless theory of location as the indices provided by Florence can only **reveal the existing state of industrial distribution** in a country. It fails to explain the causes responsible for the choice of location. It can be, thus, said that, though Florence's analysis serves as a guide for an effective planning of an economy but this theory can be called as an investigation of the 'status quo' and nothing more than it.
2. This theory fails to explain the various forces of concentration or dispersion of industries. For instance, concentration may be due to existence of external economies to the units, or some industries are migratory in nature due to the demand for their products, or tax incentives in some areas and not available in other encourage dispersal of units. All these factors, that have direct bearing on the location of industrial units, are not taken into consideration.
3. In explaining the two new concepts, in the theory – 'location factor' or 'co-efficient of localisation', the theory makes use of the political region and not industrial zones. Thus, critics believe that the choice should be economic regions, but not political regions. The co-efficient of localisation given by Florence could not be the same for all the countries as the distribution pattern of workers in each country varies as per the local conditions.

Sargent's theory is based on the number of workers for the calculation of the two concepts. But such a calculation presumes that there would be a 'given' ratio between the number of workers employed and the output of the industry. This may not be true as production techniques differ from area to area for **the same** output; and also differences in the efficiency of workers may differ in different regions.

In short, it is not logical to choose only one factor – number of workers as the sole indicator of concentration of an industry. In fact, the critics believe that a better basis of comparison would be the output in each area.

It is suggested that a judicious combination of the two theories – Alfred Weber's theory and Prof. Sargent Florence's theory would serve as a guide in framing the location planning. From the Weber's theory, it's unrealistic assumptions are to be given up. The assumption of transport relations should be given up. Instead of treating transport factor in terms of weight and distance, alternative means of transport in different areas and the existing rate schedules are to be considered. Further, technical factors of ton-miles adopted in the theory may be substituted by the actual cost of transport for the alternative potential location points.

The theory also assumes fixed labour centres which must be substituted by degree of mobility of labour in each area. As for the fixed consumption points, it is desirable that larger areas of consumption are considered and not a particular narrow regions.

The theory needs modification in terms of costs rather than merely in terms of technical factors.

With the above said modifications, the **Weber's** theory can be profitably employed for the investigation of practical problems. **Prof. Florence** has provided indices in his theory which greatly assist in the analysis of existing state of location. Even though certain limitations are there, yet the co-efficient of localisation helps the government in deciding upon the types of industries that are subject to dispersion under a scheme of regionalism.

2.4.3 August Losch's Theory of Location (Central Place Theory of Losch)

Weber's theory concentrated only on supply and cost considerations and ignored demand completely. In contrast, Losch's Theory concentrated only on demand and almost neglected supply considerations.

In his theory, therefore, Losch tried to incorporate demand by considering the size of the market and maintained that the *best location would be that which would command the largest market area, since this would bring in the highest sales revenue.*

The theory is based on the following assumptions:

- He assumed a broad homogenous plane with uniform resource endowment. It implies virtual rejection of all cost difference factors affecting industrial location.
- The theory assumes an isotropic plane, a homogenous land surface with an evenly distributed population, each having the same tastes and similar technical capabilities.
- The theory assumes identical production, identical demand curves for each buyer of each product.
- Transportation costs are proportional to distance. In such a situation, the shape and size of market area will depend on the price of the product and the rate of transport cost.

Illustration:

Let us take a simple situation in which there is only one producer who is located at a central place. He sells his product around the location point in circular bell, the extent of which depends on the economies of scale accruing to the producer and the transportation (i.e., distribution cost of the product).

The demand for the product falls with the distance.

The maximum extent of the market area for the producer is *given by the distance* when demand falls to zero because of high price for the product.

In Fig. 2.2 this is shown by OP

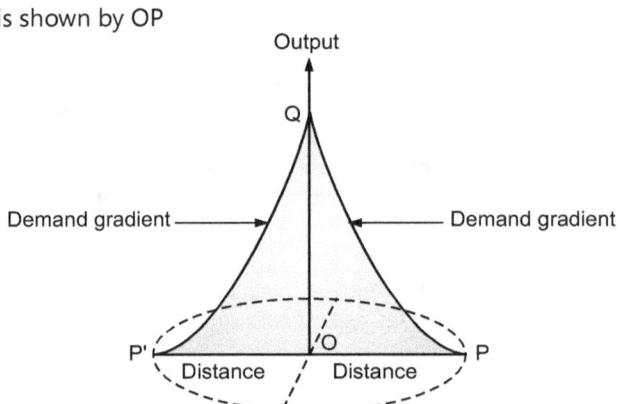

Fig. 2.2: Losch Model (Market Area of a Firm)

- The circle with OP as radius defines the market area for the producer.
- O is the location of the producer at which the demand for his product is OQ.
- The producer makes profits as the illustration shows that he is the only producer.
- The profits attract other competitors in the industry and they put up their plants in that area.
- Since there are no restrictions and resources are available, the entry of new producers gradually reduces the market area of the existing firms.
- Their markets will not continue to be circular but somehow irregular in shape.
- However, when distribution of the firms in the plain is uniform, the market area for each one of them will be hexagonal. At this stage, the profits for each firm will be minimal.
- *Each industry* will have a system of hexagons of its own.
- The superimposition of hexagons of different industries produces a common production centre surrounded by the sub-centres of productions in orderly sequence.

Critical Evaluation:
- Losch's theory is essentially a central place theory similar to Christaller's theory.
- It is a general spatial equilibrium theory. It throws no light on the factors which determine the location of individual firms.
- The assumptions of the theory (e.g., perfect competition, uniform cost and market conditions, etc) are such that the location is indeterminate.
- The major weakness of Losch's theory is rejection of cost differences.
- The theory being too much abstract in nature has limited usefulness for practical purposes.

To conclude, the objective of this chapter was to have an exposition to the problem and approaches to the industrial location analysis. Such understanding is a pre-requisite for optimal locational decision-making.

Points to Remember

- A manufacturer, while setting up a unit, has to take three inter-related decisions at the same time.
- All the conventional theories of the firm provides the rules for taking the decision on the scale of operation and technique to be adopted and gives no explanation on the location of the factory.

Factors Determining Location of Industries:

- Profit maximisation is the major goal in the choice of location of industry.
- Availability of raw materials
- Labour
- Nearness to Markets
- Transport facilities
- Power
- Site and Services
- Finance
- Natural and Climate Factors
- Personal Factors
- Strategic Factors
- External advantages
- Other factors.

Alfred Weber's Theory of Industrial Location:

- Weber's theory of location is purely deductive in its approach.
- The influencing factors in location of industries are :
  - (a) Regional factors (factors influencing inter-regional location of industries).
  - (b) Agglomerating factors (factors influencing intra-regional location).
- Weber's theory is based on many assumptions :
  - (a) The industrial unit has to choose such location that its total transportation costs are minimum.
- The key factors that determine transportation costs are :
  - (a) The weight to be transported, and
  - (b) The distance to be covered.
- **Material Index** (MI) is defined as :
  MI = Weight of localised material/Weight of finished products.
- Location Weight = Weight of material and products/Weight of products.
- An agglomerative factor is an advantage of production or marketing which results from concentration of production.
- A deglomerative factor is cheapening of production resulting from decentralisation of production.

- 'Co-efficient of manufacture' is the ratio of manufacturing cost to locational weight.
- 'Index of manufacture' is the proportion of manufacturing costs to the total weight of the product.
- Weber's theory has been severely criticized due to the assumptions on which it is based.

Sargent Florence's Theory:

- Florence theory is an inductive analysis of location of industries.
- 'Location factor' is an index of the degree of concentration of an industry in a particular region.
- 'Co-efficient of localisation' shows the propensity of an industry for concentration or dispersion.
- Florence's analysis serves as a guide for an effective planning but it can be called as an investigation of the 'status quo'.
- All the forces of concentration or dispersion of industries are not explained in the theory.
- The theory used political region as its base rather than industrial zone.
- Critics suggest that a judicious combination of the two theories would serve as a guide in framing the locational planning.

August Losch's Theory Of Location

- Losch tried to incorporate demand by considering the size of the market and maintained that the *best location would be that which would command the largest market area, since this would bring in the highest sales revenue.*

Questions for Discussion

1. Explain in brief the factors determining the location of Industries.
2. Critically evaluate Weber's theory of location of industries.
3. Examine the criticisms levelled against the Weber's theory. Point out the possible modifications to this pure theory.
4. Give detailed information on the factors influencing the location of industries.
5. Explain the theory of location of industries as given by Sargent Florence.
6. What are the criticisms levelled against the Florence theory?
7. Explain the dynamics of industrial location.
8. Discuss the recent trends in the location of industries.
9. Illustrate the different techniques used in decision-making of a site for an industrial unit.

■ ■ ■

Chapter **3**...

Industrial Productivity

Contents ...

Learning Objectives ...

At the end of the Chapter, you will be able:

- To learn about Industrial Productivity and the factors influencing it
- To be aware of the measures adopted by the Indian Government to improve Industrial Productivity

3.1 Introduction

Industrial productivity is closely linked with economic growth and is essential for raising production per unit. It furnishes a significant tool of economic analysis.

Productivity has its importance at various levels - be it at the local, national or international level. Productivity is different from production and can be measured. In fact, its indices are useful in examining the effectiveness of the various schemes of rationalisation and scientific management.

Production has become a key issue with planners, policy makers and other professionals. Economic growth has come to be firmly linked with gains in productivity. Capital formation plays an important role in the growth process. Additional capital facilitates a more rapid rate of economic development yet, capital by itself is insufficient. Sustained economic growth requires a steady rise in productivity.

Technological progress including the upgradation of physical and human resources provides the basis or precondition for continuous economic growth.

Low productivity is a feature common to most sectors in developing economies. Added to it is the problem of higher rate of population growth which makes it difficult to raise per capita income from present low levels.

The historical growth record of contemporary developed nations reveals a high rate of increase in total factor productivity – particularly a rise in human resource productivity. This contributes to a considerable surplus and a high per capita income. In the light of the above, a negative index of productivity in developing countries is a great concern. This trend has to be reversed immediately.

In recent years there have been a considerable amount of discussions and theoretical analysis of the concept of 'productivity'. This term has been differently defined by different thinkers.

3.2 Meaning, Definitions and Measurement of Industrial Productivity

3.2.1 Meaning of Industrial Productivity

Industrial production is a measure of output of the industrial sector of the economy.

Production of any commodity is as a result of the combined efforts of the different factors of production such as land, labour, capital and enterprise. Technically, these factors are termed as 'inputs' and the resultant product is the 'output'.

Productivity is a measure of the rate at which output of goods and services are produced per unit of 'input' (labour, capital, raw materials etc).

It is calculated as the ratio of the amount of output produced to some measure of the amount of input used.

Depending on the context and the selection of input and output measures, productivity calculations can have different interpretations.

(a) Improving productivity can be in relation to economising on the use of inputs, for example, adopting efficient production processes that minimise waste.

(b) Improving productivity can be in relation to yielding more output, for example, using resources in activities or technologies that generate more output.

However, productivity is a 'supply-side' measure, i.e. relating to technical production relationships between inputs and outputs.

Thus, *productivity is a ratio between the total output and the input of resources used in the process of any economic activity.*

Although, productivity is influenced by different factors but in general discussion, productivity focus more on *labour force*. Thus, in a narrow sense, when the term 'productivity' is used without any particular qualifications, it is understood as productivity of labour. This is because that productivity of labour influences the cost of production and prices of goods. Labour productivity determines the wage rates, level of income and standard of living of labourers.

Productivity of labour is measured in terms of 'output per man-hour' or 'output per unit of labour time'.

As said earlier, in the broadest sense, the sum total of all 'inputs' and the sum total of all 'outputs' resulting out of it is taken into account to measure the productivity in the economy. And, thus, increasing productivity implies more efficient use of all the factors of production than before and thus reducing to a great extent the wastage of various factors of production (or inputs).

3.2.2 Definitions of Industrial Productivity

So far no clear definition of the term productivity has been given. But, some of the definitions are as given below:

- **International Labour Office (ILO):** *"The ratio between the output and one of the factors of input is generally known as productivity of the factor considered."*
- **Prof. S. C. Kuchhal:** *"Productivity implies development of an attitude of mind and a constant urge to find cheaper, quicker, easier and safer ways of doing a job, manufacturing a product and providing a service. It aims at the maximum utilisation of resources for yielding as many goods and services as possible, of the kinds most wanted by consumers, at the lowest possible cost".*
- **Evan Claugue:** *"Productivity expresses the overall efficiency with which our industries perform."*
- **J. M. S. Risk:** *"Productivity as a physical ratio related to quantity of goods produced or service given in comparison with the quantity of resource consumed".* Variety of resources used when converted into money terms still represents all physical factors.
- **R. W. Fenske** defines productivity in five different ways : "Productivity is *(i) a form of efficiency, (ii) is utilisation of resources or effectiveness of utilisation of resources, (iii) it is a ratio rather than a phenomenon, (iv) is a measure of some kind (rather than a variable requiring measurement), (v) it is rate of return (primarily in monetary terms)".*
- **Central Board for Workmen's Education:**
  The word 'productivity' can be explained as under:
  1. Productivity means getting more out of the existing resources.
  2. Productivity means elimination of waste.
  3. Productivity is an effort to save time, energy, power and money to achieve higher production at lower cost.
  4. Productivity primarily stands for more output from lesser inputs.
  Different thinkers have defined the term productivity differently, yet the one given by ILO is considered as the most suitable one.
- **Evan Claugue's** definition makes it difficult to measure productivity quantitatively.
- **Risk's** definition does not help in comparing two units where the money value changes due to the exchange rate.

- As for ILO's definition, **Prof. S. C. Kuchhal** comments that *"Popularity of ILO's definition undoubtedly rests on the widespread interest in labour saving as such a saving can affect prices, jobs, wages and even a nation's military security and level of living"*.

The most important reasons *why labour is used as the commonest factor in measuring productivity are:*

(i) It is easy to precise to measure the units of labour inputs as compared to other inputs like materials, capital etc. Thus, productivity can be very easily measured in terms of output per man, output per man-hour or output per unit of labour time;

(ii) Labour input is universally applied to all types of plants, process and productions;

(iii) It has become a common practice to link wages with the productivity.

However, consideration of the concept of productivity with reference to the labour only suffers from the following *limitations:*

(i) The output ascertained per man-hour does not measure the productive efficiency as a whole or even as the productive contribution of the labour.

(ii) An increase in output per man-hour may or may not be desirable. Moreover, it may not reduce the unit labour cost.

(iii) If increase in output per man-hour is accompanied by only a proportionate increase in hourly wage rate, production costs are more likely to increase than to remain unchanged in capital-intensive industries like Iron and Steel Industry.

(iv) Output should not be considered in terms of intangible work, but the aspects such as pleasure and work satisfaction which the workers derived from the work should also be considered. So also, under the input considerations, due weightage should also be given to the factors such as fatigue, effect on health, monotony, ability to enjoy the leisure time, recreation etc. The measurement of such factors is difficult and may result in subjective considerations.

3.2.3 Scope and Importance of Productivity Measurement

Each nation is interested in growth in order to solve economic problems of its ever growing population and raise their standard of living. It is true that since productivity indicates the magnitude of changes in the economic activity, its scope embraces all the facets of economic welfare.

Productivity reflects the rate of energy of production. The macro-economic aspect of average productivity means international indicators of productivity for comparison and remedial action at appropriate levels; and the micro-economic aspect of productivity takes consideration of various industries in a country including inter-industrial, inter-regional, inter-departmental etc.

During the recent years much trust has been put on productivity studies as objective and scientific indicators of the change in the economic and industrial organisation of the country. Indeed, productivity indices have been used for a variety of objectives at different levels of economic activity.

Productivity is a *statistical measure* and serves as an effective tool of economic analysis. Let us discuss the **significance** of productivity measurement.

1. Productivity growth **contributes to growth in output, income and living standards**. Let us see how:

    Productivity growth = Output growth – Input growth

    Rearranging,   Output growth = Input growth + Productivity growth

    i.e., input growth and productivity growth both contribute to output growth.

    If output is measured as value-added then output growth is equal to income growth.

    Thus, productivity growth leads to income growth in an economy.

2. At a firm or industry level, the benefits of productivity growth can be distributed in various ways, such as:

    *   To the workforce through better wages and work conditions;
    *   To shareholders and superannuation funds through increased profits and dividend distributions;
    *   To customers through lower prices;
    *   To the environment through more stringent environmental protection; and
    *   To governments through increases in tax payments, to be used in funding social and environmental programmes.

3. Productivity growth is important to the firm because it means it can meet its obligations to workers, shareholders and governments (taxes and regulation), and still remain competitive or even improve its competitiveness in the market place.

4. The indices of productivity **serve as indicators of the changes** in economic and industrial organisation of a country. It can be said that the productivity indices serve as 'barometers' of the country's industrial and economic growth. It points out to the changes taking place in the growth of the economy. In this way, these indices can help to predict and forecast industrial and economic growth.

5. Labour **productivity** indices assist in formulating the wage policy and conditions of work in industrial establishments.

6. Labour productivity indices are significant **to economic policy-makers** to know the effects of new schemes introduced. It is useful to entrepreneurs and trade union leaders to evolve and pursue such realistic policies that would be more effective and successful.

7. Labour productivity is used for **evaluating effectiveness of the various schemes** of rationalisation and scientific management, at the plant level. For example, if a new scheme of labour welfare is introduced in a plant, it is the labour productivity indices that are useful in evaluating their impact. Productivity measurement helps to find out whether a new labour saving device or introduction of a new wage pattern has responded to the need of the industry. In short, these indices are effective instruments of management policy formulation and decision-making.

8. Productivity indices are **useful in formulating fiscal and taxation policies**, in estimating the degree of protection to any particular industry, in adopting labour welfare measures or social insurance schemes, in forecasting economic trends, in helping formulate policies of allocating resources into different channels.

9. Productivity indices are very significant as **they allow comparisons :**
   (a) Between different units (or enterprises) of any particular industry;
   (b) Between industries in other countries;
   (c) The indices of productivity make the progress being made over the entire industry very clear.

10. Influence of technological changes on the volume of production is also measured with the help of productivity. According to **Prof. S. C. Kuchhal**, productivity helps in 'allocating the national, financial and human resources which would maximise the national welfare'.

To conclude, one can quote the utility of productivity in **Prof. S. C. Kuchhal's** words, *"Their utility is not merely confined to analytical statisticians and industrial engineers who are mainly interested either in ascertaining productivity trends for whole industries or nations or in measuring performances at low levels; they are equally useful as tools of economic analysis and appraisal to statesmen, businessmen and labour union leaders who wish to pursue a more realistic policy based on observed facts."*

Difference between Production and Productivity:

Though both the terms 'production' and 'productivity' are closely linked with each other, there is a clear difference between the two terms.

'Production' refers to the output that can be increased even by installing more machines and other resources.

On the other hand, *'productivity'* refers to a worker's output per unit of time.

Let us illustrate the difference between the two terms. The two factories A and B with the same type and number of machines and with all other factors of production exactly the same, the number of workers being the same, and if factory A produces 50 units of a commodity per day and factory B produces 100 units of the same commodity per day, it would imply that productivity of labour in factory B is higher than in factory A.

Though higher productivity leads to higher production, higher production does not necessarily mean higher productivity.

In an industrial unit, production can be increased by employing more **of all resources** financial, manual, capital etc. On the other hand, **productivity** can be possible **by utilising more effectively** the existing volume of inputs to **secure** more output or getting the same output by reducing the inputs.

In short, productivity is related to efficiency of the organisation and the management. With the same illustration of the two factories A and B, we can say that with all the factors remaining the same in the two plants and now if there is an increase in labour productivity in plant A and not in factory B, then production in factory A will be higher than in factory B. Alternatively, if in factory A, by reducing the number of workers, keeping other factors of production the same as before, production remains the same as before, it can be said that productivity of labour has increased in factory A.

According to **Prof. S. C. Kuchhal**, *"Production in itself does not raise the standard of living. It must be accompanied by increase of real income which can be possible only through increase in productivity."*

Distinction between Production and Productivity are as follows:

Production	Productivity
1. Production is concerned with the end results of the contribution of various factors in the share of volume, value of quantity of goods and services turned out by a plant.	1. Productivity views the volume, value of quantity of production in relation to the resources utilised in the production of such goods and services.
2. Production, thus, represents the total volume of output produced or manufactured.	2. Productivity shows the efficiency of the production unit.
3. Production is an absolute measure.	3. Productivity is a relative measure.

With reference to the inter-relationship between productivity and production, the following statements can be understood:

1. Productivity remaining unchanged; production will increase with an increase in inputs.

2. Inputs spent or used up remaining unchanged; production will increase with an increase in productivity.

3. Production changes (increase or decrease) when both productivity and inputs change i.e. increase or decrease.

4. Production will increase, if increase in productivity is more than offsets the effect of reduction in inputs.

5. Production will fall, if the effect of increase in inputs is more than offset by decline in productivity.

Elements of Productivity:

Achieving high productivity implies obtaining as much output as possible from a given number of units of the factors of production. *Three elements* **that influence productivity are capital, technology and people.**

1. Capital Resource: Capital is scarce in developing countries. Hence, these countries have to make judicious and discriminate use of capital. However, where consistency in quality or reduction of strain on workers is involved, automation is desirable. Most developing nations gets caught in a dilemma whether to use a highly capital intensive technology to improve productivity or use techniques which result in greater employment generation. What needs to be done is to identify those areas where application of capital – intensive technologies yield higher surpluses which then be reinvested to create more employment. Another key decision that has to be taken is about the economic size of volume sensitive areas. This is crucial as the market developing countries may not be large enough to warrant very big establishments. Inspite of the scarcity of capital, we find output per unit of capital declining in most developing economies. Long gestation periods, under-utilisation of capacity and poor maintenance are some of the contributing factors.

2. Technology: Technology is a rapidly changing with continuous innovations and new processes either to increase the output or improve the quality of the products. Today, there are constant efforts carried on to cut costs and improve quality through technological innovations. Production technologies are constantly improving with better tools. Technological breakthrough has taken place not only in the design of products but also in the processes. However, most technological breakthrough has taken place in few advanced countries. Today, many of our industries continue to use obsolete designs and outdated production technologies. This obviously has an adverse impact on the productivity and efficiency in the use of resources.

3. Human resource: The third essential input which influences productivity is the human resource. It has been recognised in the world over that productivity through people is one of the attributes that characteristics high achieving countries and companies. This is even more relevant in developing countries where human resource is abundant and wages are comparatively lower.

Undoubtedly, it is difficult to answer this question as to which factor/element is most important – capital, technology or people? In reality, all elements of productivity are vital.

With recent experiences in developed and developing countries, it is essential to place a greater emphasis on productivity through people. The failure to recognise and motivate human resources has been the main cause of our failure to achieve higher levels of productivity.

A brief mention of the Japanese economic miracle will highlight many points. Post-war conditions in Japan were worse than the conditions prevalent in most developing countries today. There was wide-spread poverty. War time devastation had crippled most industries and they were characterised by poor productivity and poor quality output. The scarcity of capital and in absence of natural resources in Japan left no choice to their people but to work hard for survival and upliftment. Japan made heavy investments in development and in educational system and this contributed to the rapid economic growth subsequently.

3.2.4 Measurement of Productivity

Productivity *is a ratio between output and input.*

In symbolic terms, Productivity = Net Output ÷ Effort Input.

In case labour productivity is to be measured then it is a ratio between output and labour.

Symbolically,   Labour Productivity = Net Output ÷ Number of workers; or

Labour Productivity = Net Output ÷ Number of man hours.

Further, if the productivity of capital is to be measured, then it is the ratio between output and capital.

Symbolically,   Capital Productivity = Net Output ÷ Net Capital Employed.

As stated earlier, in actual practice, labour is selected as the unit of output while calculating productivity. In India too, *productivity is referred to more as labour productivity.* Thinkers also point out that as labour is an abundant factor in India (that might depress the industrial productivity) hence, productivity should be measured in terms of raw materials, capital resources, machine capacity etc.

Indices of Productivity (Different Measures of Productivity)

As productivity measures the output per unit of input, theoretically there are as many indices of productivity as there are inputs:

(i) **Labour Productivity:** Labour productivity is obtained by dividing the gross value added by the average daily employment.

$$\text{Labour Productivity} = \frac{\text{Gross value added}}{\text{Average daily employment}}$$

where,   Valued added = Output

The gross value added (i.e. numerator) is obtained by subtracting raw material inputs and fuel, electricity and lubricants consumed from the ex-factory value of the output. Depreciation is not deducted. The average daily employment (i.e. denominator) is obtained by the total attendance of the persons in all the shifts on all working days and dividing it by the number of days worked.

(ii) **Capital Productivity:** It is obtained by dividing the gross value added by the fixed capital.

$$\text{Capital Productivity} = \frac{\text{Gross value added}}{\text{Fixed capital}}$$

In the fixed capital investments is considered land, buildings, plant, machinery etc. The working capital is excluded because under inflationary business conditions, the components of working capital such as inventories, receivables, cash holdings etc. are more often determined by the supply and the market expectations rather than by the purely technological pipeline requirements of the working capital.

(iii) **Raw Materials and Fuel Input Productivity :** It is obtained by dividing the gross ex-factory value of output by the combined value of inputs like raw materials, fuel, electricity, lubricants etc.

$$\text{Raw Material and Fuel Input Productivity} = \frac{\text{Gross ex-factory value of output}}{\text{Combined value of raw-material, fuel etc. inputs}}$$

(iv) **Total Factor Productivity Index:** It is a ratio between output and the sum of combined inputs of labour and capital.

$$\text{Factory Productivity Index} = \frac{V_t}{W_o L_t + R_o C_t}$$

where,

V_t = Gross value added in year 't',

W_o = Base year wage rate,

R_o = Base year return on capital,

L_t and C_t = Labour and Capital inputs in year 't'.

The indices of productivity focus on the measurement of output and various types of inputs and thus they help in determining which particular output – input comparisons are most relevant in evaluating the performances of various operations and units of a concern to management and to interpret such findings with regard to the influence of internally controllable and externally imposed factors.

Problems or Limitations in Productivity Measurement: There are certain limitations in the measurement of industrial productivity:

(i)   In case of finished products of homogenous nature, measurement of productivity is easier. However, it is quite difficult to measure productivity of certain industries producing *heterogeneous goods* such as electric, engineering, chemical industries etc.

(ii)   Limitations and difficulties are faced when measuring productivity of *service industries* like banking, insurance etc., as the output cannot be directly measurable in terms of physical units.

(iii)   There arises *technical difficulty* involved in the measurement of output. Generally, output is viewed as the volume of finished product and little attention is paid to the work-in-progress which is also a result of use of 'inputs' as used in a finished product.

(iv)   It is difficult to take into account much *invisible and intangible output* or associated services which may have no bearing on current production while measuring productivity, as seen in the case of maintenance of scientific and industrial research laboratories, market research bureau's etc.

(v)   Though measurement of labour productivity is the most important component of industrial productivity it *lacks certain measures of precision and clarity*. Labour productivity can be measured on the basis of man-hours worked or the total number of workers employed. However, the use of both these concepts of labour suffers from a few limitations. For instance, the man-hours concept does not consider the qualitative differences in the character and composition of labour. And, if we take the number of workers employed for the purpose, it is difficult to fix any specific weights for all categories of labour. (Different major categories of labour include male, female and child labour. Child labour forms only an insignificant part of the total labour employed. Further, these categories cannot be combined on a uniform basis).

(vi)   The *compilation of international comparison is a highly complex* and difficult task. The difficulty in selecting a suitable yardstick for measuring productivity is the cause for such a situation. For example, in certain countries the real net product per man-hour worked is taken as a measuring rod but while doing so depreciation for national stock of capital is not statistically measurable. In certain other countries productivity of capital is taken. In the intervening periods of comparison the price changes will come up and they are to be eliminated. The exchange rates that are fixed in the periods of comparison do not reveal the relative change over time.

3.3 Factors Affecting Industrial Productivity

There are different, numerous and complex factors that influence productivity of an industrial sector in an economy. But, it is highly difficult to accurately measure how much each of the factor contributes to increasing productivity. The reason for this is that no one factor by itself can noticeably increase productivity. It is generally the simultaneous operation of various other factors. It can also be observed that a favourable effect of one factor on industrial productivity might be written-off by the operation of some other unfavourable factor or factors at the same time.

Factors influencing industrial productivity can be classified under two broad categories - *external factors and internal factors.* A detailed discussion of the numerous factors determining productivity is given below:

1. Natural Factors: Such factors include geographical location, climate and availability of water and mineral resources. All these factors have a deep impact on industrial productivity.

Geographical conditions determine productivity in the extractive industries. For example, tropical climate generally unfavourably influences the physical strength and thus bears an unfavourable effect on industrial productivity.

If the country is endowed with abundant industrial raw materials of excellent quality, it has a favourable impact on industries using those natural resources. In fact, natural factors affect directly and indirectly the productivity of an industry in an economy. For instance, if crude oil is found in abundance and also gas or sources of hydro-electricity will certainly produce favourable effects on industrial productivity in the country. In other industries like grain-milling, hosiery, soap-making, confectionary etc. the geographical; geological and physical factors exercise little influence on productivity. Further, in case of agricultural industries, climate and geographical factors play a vital role in influencing industrial productivity.

2. Technological Factors: Technical factor is the single most powerful factor with the greatest impact on industrial productivity. The simplest example can be quoted   from the comparison of production of cloth by a worker with the aid of a handloom, a power loom and automatic loom; one can notice the impact of technological factor on productivity.

"The application of motive power and mechanical improvement to the processes of production has accelerated the pace of industrialisation to an unprecedented degree, and has given us the vision of the vast and unexplored frontiers that still lie ahead of us in the realm of science and technology."

The most dominant factors that have contributed to the spectacular advances in industrial productivity are the application of mechanical power, introduction of highly specialised and semi-automatic and automatic machines, more efficient co-ordination, improvement in the production process and greater degree of specialisation both of work and output.

Technological advances accompanied by increasing skills and capabilities of handling complex machines could allow Ford to produce from six cars per month to a car per minute.

Even when we know technical progress has a favourable impact on industrial productivity, it is difficult to measure exactly how much increase there has taken place in industrial productivity due to technological progress.

As compared to developed nations, developing countries like India, suffer from relatively low productivity and one of the major reasons is obsolete machinery, lack of spare parts, inadequate skills for machine-handling, inadequate power supply, neglect of research and development which are the foundation of technological progress.

3. Financial Factors: Productivity increases due to technological innovations. But it is difficult to adopt such innovations in the absence of adequate financial facilities.

It can be well said that industrial productivity depends to a great extent on technological improvements and innovations and adoption of such measures in turn depends on the availability of sufficient financial resources.

It is only by investing vast amounts in up-to-date machinery, well-stocked spare parts and other inventories and R & D, that industrial productivity can be increased. For example, the jute textile industry has for long been faced with the problem of obsolete and worn-out plant and machinery. The industry did not accumulate internal resources for modernisation of plant and machinery. In short, where the capital is relatively abundant and the supply of labour is comparatively scarce, the movement of mechanisation would accelerate industrial productivity.

4. Labour Force: It is the skilled labour force that has been a major contributing factor in the transformation of a static past into the dynamic present. In the times of economic stable or upheaval conditions, the strength of a nation depends upon the inherent qualities of its labour force. No spectacular gains in the industrial progress have been made in developing nations due to lack of proper facilities necessary for the upkeep of body and mind of the labour force. There has been noticed a positive correlation between the standard of living of a nation and the skill that the country's labour force can acquire. Other factors that influence the quality of the labour force and bear a great impact on determining industrial productivity are wage payments, working conditions, degree of mechanisation of work and specialisation, material used in production, tools supplied etc.

5. Size of the Industry: One of an important factor that determines labour productivity is economies of large scale. When other factors like technology, labour etc. remain at the same level, large-scale unit should be more efficient than a small-scale unit. This is because a large-size industrial unit enjoys the economies of large-scale such as advantageous position in obtaining the supplies of raw material at lower prices, enjoys specialisation of managerial ability, secures greater economies in the marketing of finished product and in utilising the by-products and in raising the required finance. Large-scale units are more in position to spend substantial sums of money on research and development which leads to a greater productivity.

6. Managerial Factors: With the growing complexity of the production units, managerial factors have come to play a very dominating role in determining productivity of different industrial units.

An industrial leader with a grand but practical vision, with determination and dedication, with ability to inspire confidence and motivation in workers can make a great difference to industrial productivity. Examples of **J. R. Tata, Ford** show what industrial leaders with vision and determination can achieve.

Under the present system of industrial production, management has to perform a wide variety of functions i.e. decision-making, organising, planning, directing, controlling, staffing, co-ordinating etc. A manager's job is to increase productivity, which is the key to prosperity.

It has been rightly said that "never before in the history of industrial development was there a great need of energetic, enterprising, fore-sighted managerial talents imbued with the spirit of adventure of qualities of judgment, imagination and vigilance, as is today; for the individual units are destined to sink or swim with those who guide and govern their destinies."

6. Institutional Factors: Sociological and cultural factors play a great role in influencing industrial productivity. If the existing economic and social institutions are not conducive to improvements, it would be difficult to anticipate substantial gains in industrial productivity, even in the presence of adequate amount of raw material and abundant supply of technology progress. A society ridden with caste system and having barriers in assigning duties and obligations to each caste and hampering horizontal and vertical mobility of labour would have an adverse effect on industrial productivity. On the other hand, widespread industrial culture among people such as intense desire to earn a rising level of income, raise one's standard of living, discipline, hard work, desire to acquire modern skills and scientific approach etc. would have a favourable impact on industrial productivity.

Developed nations are enjoying high industrial productivity due to their progressive social institutions and cultural values. Developing countries like India are still having feudal institutions and medieval value-system and attitudes developed when agriculture was the prime occupation. A sound industrial structure with high industrial productivity cannot be built on feudal social institutions and value-system.

In short, to raise industrial productivity, appropriate social and cultural institutions must be established side by side. For instance, a traditional education system based on religion and literary learning must be substituted by an education system where science and technology have an important place.

7. Government Policies: Government's financial; tariff, taxation and external trade policies bear a great influence on industrial productivity. For example, a high rate of depreciation allowance can help adoption of high technology. In India, the practice of allowing only 10 percent of depreciation on the basis of historical costs has obstructed the adoption of modern technology and has negatively affected the industrial productivity. Again, tax concessions or lower custom duty on imports of the latest technology would impart greater industrial productivity.

On one hand, too much protection given to any industry encourages monopoly at home and adversely affects productivity, on the other hand the emergence of competitive markets lead to increased industrial productivity.

Government's various policies can go a long way in creating an environment of higher industrial productivity.

For example, the New Economic Policy of 1991 which introduced the concept of broad-banding encouraged production, allowed product-mix on market demand in large number of items such as motorised two wheelers , motorised four-wheelers, petro-chemical, fertilizer industry etc.

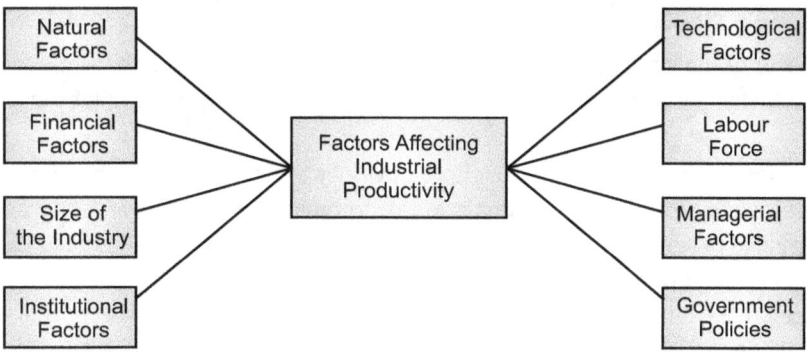

Fig. 3.1: Factors Affecting Industrial Productivity

Misconceptions of Productivity:

In **Solomon Fabricant's** words, "Productivity is a subject surrounded by considerable confusion."

From the *labourer's side* it can be said that the workers generally oppose implementation of productivity schemes in industrial units.

They believe that with productivity schemes implemented they have to work more hard. Thus, trade union leaders associate the concept of productivity with heavier work-load, more intensive efforts and higher profits to management than before.

But workers need to be convinced that productivity schemes when implemented would mean better working conditions, less fatigue and less effort.

The union leaders also believe that productivity schemes lead to displacement of workers. Thus, mention of the word 'productivity' immediately gives rise to fears among workers and trade union leaders about unemployment.

But there is no logical co-relation between measures for improving labour productivity and unemployment of labour. In fact, it has been observed that where labour productivity is low that the level of employment of labour is generally low and that of unemployment high.

Economic progress means change in old processes of production and adoption of more efficient and cost-reducing processes requiring newer skills. In such cases, in less developing countries like India, with labour surplus and with vast amount of unemployment, intensive attempts should be made to keep to the minimum such displaced workers by process such as gradually phasing out redundant workers as they retire or leave voluntarily.

Further, another misconception about productivity schemes is that management alone benefit by such schemes. This misconception can be cleared by adopting productivity improvement schemes with the co-operation and coordination of the workers.

3.4 Measures Adopted by the Indian Government to Improve Productivity

Industrial productivity has its own tools. There are various factors that influence and can increase productivity of labour. Some of the important tools of improving labour productivity are:

(i)   It is possible to increase labour productivity *by improving industrial relations.*

(ii) By *providing training* to workers and taking measures to *improve labour welfare,* one can raise productivity. The simple explanation for this measure is that a satisfied and contented labourer will work more efficiently.

(iii) To increase labour productivity, it is essential that there arises a mutual agreement between management and workers with respect to *distribution of benefits* of the rise in labour productivity.

(iv) Scientific management techniques should be used. In recent years, management science has developed to a great extent and by introducing modern methods of organisation and *adopting modern scientific techniques and management practices,* labour productivity can be increased.

(v)   Work, time and motion studies should be carried out to scientifically determine better and quicker ways of doing a job. It would help in producing the same output by employing lesser number of workers and lesser working hours. In other words, by simplification, *specialisation and standardisation,* labour productivity can be raised.

(vi) Steps should be taken to *improve plant lay-out, material handling* and have better internal management in a plant. Such steps would increase labour productivity.

(vii) It is possible to create an atmosphere in a factory that would motivate workers to put in better efforts and thus raise labour productivity. Such motivation would be by *providing modern training courses to those in the personnel department* who handle workers.

(viii) Motivation to produce more is necessary and such motivation among workers is when *wages are linked to the productivity of workers.*

(ix) Linking not only the wages but incentive bonus, allowances etc. which, with increase in labour productivity, *promise higher wages and standard of living* serves as the most effective way of raising labour productivity.

(x) Labour productivity can be raised by *comprehensive and complete planning* and introducing production, quality and cost controls.

(xi) More *social welfare schemes* should be introduced in the industry to get more co-operations of the workers.

(xii) *Better human relations* should be developed.

In short, there are different tools of industrial productivity, which aim at bringing efficiency.

Managerial Role in Improving Productivity:

Most organisations tend to focus on upgrading measurable skills and introducing new technology. But these remain mere cosmetic exercises. What is more relevant is the upgrading of the human resources within the organisation. Therefore, Human Resource Development (HRD) programme needs to harness the creative energy in all individuals in the organisation.

For upgrading human resource, the management should introduce a style and culture that promotes creativity. Engendering creativity may involve a partial rejection of the set patterns in an organisation. Such a situation may call for more dynamic and supportive role by the management.

In generating creativity it is required that there would be persistent and subtle attempts at controlling the officers and on the other hand, the management needs to keep an eye on the issue of creativity and productivity by conducting regular exercises like brain storming and group discussions.

The normal mode of creativity enhancing exercises includes the following:

(a) **Borrowing New Ideas from Others:** This would involve taking advice from consultant on particular problems.

(b) **Employing Creative People:** The creative people would act as free thinkers for the company. Good companies are known for such practices. Akio Morita of Sony used to induct a female employee who would give her views on the "looks" of Sony products.

(c) **Training the Workforce to be Creative:** Here again Sony had set an example by encouraging its employees to contribute creative ideas. In 1986, the company received 2,650,000 suggestions from employees, of which 96 per cent were considered valid.

To appreciate creativity properly, one should remember that there are times when each one of us have flashes of inspiration – the desire to do something extraordinary. Here again, the role of management becomes crucial in encouraging the workforce to do that extra bit.

There are several factors that inhibit the development of an individual's latent creativity energy – such as the present education system, the role of parents, teachers and the stress levels in different facets of life. Any HRD manager has to keep all these factors in mind while charting out the HRD programme.

(d) **Research-Based Evidence: Alex F. Osborn**, a leader in the field of creative thinking, has studied the principles adopted by natural creators. He confirms that creativity, as a predictable process, can be learnt and practised to make it a natural part of thinking.

The courses conducted in colleges and industries have shown that latent creativity can be developed. It has been observed that those who undergo course training of creativity fair better than who do not and they exhibit confidence in airing fresh and useful ideas.

To conclude, creativity brings about changes in work culture and also generates a series of opposite ideas. Some could use creativity to cover-up their overall inefficiency. Management should be alert to such deviations. They should firmly intervene when the creativity of its workforce becomes negative in its effect.

However, the most important point to understand is that management must accept creativity as an essential tool to progress that cannot be left to chance.

Productivity in India:

Productivity in India is by and large, not very satisfactory. The causes for low industrial productivity in India are as follows:

1. **Obsolete plant and machinery**, poor production facilities and devices cause low productivity. For example, modernisation is long overdue in cause of a number of cotton textile, jute and sugar mills.

2. **Poor supervision and lack of motivation** are also responsible for low productivity. The ILO team has pointed out that one of the reasons for poor quality is that some management does not pay for suitable supervision; as a result workers' inefficiency is not corrected.

3. In India, large numbers of industrial units are **of uneconomic size.**

4. **Professionalisation of management and application of scientific management** principles can make a major contribution towards increasing industrial productivity. But, India has yet to go a long way in this direction. For example, an observation done by the working party for the Cotton Textile Industry (1952) pointed out that the take-over of several textiles mills by new entrepreneurs were with no experience and aptitude for the management of industrial units.

5. **The bad working condition is** also an important cause for low productivity. The ILO team has observed that considering the conditions are expected to work, it would not be fair to blame the workers for going out, now and then, for a spell of fresh air. Labour productivity can be considerably increased by providing healthy environment.

6. In India, industries may, enjoy a **sheltered market** or a seller's market. Industrialists enjoying protection have not been very keen to increase their operational inefficiency.

7. Due to **general poverty and under nourishment**, productivity of labour tends to be low. Lack of education and training leads to how productivity. Poor living conditions, unhealthy employer-employee relations, workers have no motivation to work sincerely and hard.

8. **Paucity of funds** is regarded as one of the important factor hindering modernisation.

9. **Rationalisation and automation** have not made much progress. Surplus labour, paucity of funds, uncertainties related to government policies have been obstacles to rationalisation and automation.

10. Indian society is still **tradition-minded.** Unfavourable social attitude towards change and lack of risk bearing attitude still stands in the way of improving productivity.

Role of Government in Improving Productivity:

Industrial productivity is affected by external and internal factors. The management of an enterprise can exercise full control over internal factors. However, external factors are beyond the control of the management as they are mainly influenced by monetary as well as fiscal policies of the government.

Efforts are thus necessary at government level to create a favourable atmosphere for industries so that their productivity can be increased in the long-run.

Government is expected to take initiative in establishing the necessary institutions which would take care of the factors affecting productivity. It should lay down favourable policies and regulations for industries.

Certain positive measures that can be undertaken by the government which are as follows:

1. **Establishment of Institutions:** Technical institutions for productivity improvement should be established both at national as well as at regional levels. These institutions should devise measure and provide training to entrepreneurs. There should be an apex body for co-ordinating the functions of all regional, technical and professional bodies in the country.

These institutions can conduct short-term courses of productivity improvement. Besides doing research in productivity improvement these institutions can also impart training in industrial engineering and techno-managerial services, since these have a direct bearing on industrial productivity.

2. **Educational System:** Productivity improvement, being a national policy, should be given due importance in the educational system so that it can encourage favourable attitude for productivity in people's conscience from an early stage.

   For this suitable curriculum can be introduced in the field of technical education. Emphasis should be laid on full utilisation of resources. Arrangements should be made to educate the managerial personnel and the workers employed in industrial establishments regarding productivity and its importance.

3. **Liaison Services:** The government should function as a *link* by bringing together the representatives of various interests and impress upon them the necessity and urgency of increasing efficiency and productivity, thus creating a spirit of co-operation in industrial field.

   The government can play a constructive role of eliminating the fear of exploitation especially among the workers by bringing management and workers together to drop their mutual distrust and work for common cause of increasing productivity.

4. **Conducive Climate:** The government should create a climate that is conducive towards productivity improvement. For example, carry on productivity campaigns, organise seminars, undertake publications of productivity material etc. Productivity consciousness should be kept alive so that it becomes a part of the thinking of the industrialists and of the working community.

5. **Data Collection:** Government can create a special cell for collection, objective interpretation and dissemination of data pertaining to productivity and the factors influencing it.

   The department should construct productive indices or ratios of different industries which would be helpful for inter-company as well as inter-industry comparisons. Similarly, national indices should be published periodically which would serve as standard ratios for the purpose of comparison of performance of individual organisations.

6. **Strong Public Sector:** In India, public sector enterprises co-exist with those in the private sector. Such government-run enterprises should be developed as models of productivity for private sector industries. Since government can afford to finance research and development programmes for boosting productivity, such programmes should be undertaken by it, the benefits of which can be extended to the private sector industries.

7. **Economic Policies:** The government should adopt economic policies that encourage productivity. Stability of favourable economic environment is most essential for the maintenance of productivity improvement efforts. Development and mobilisation of resources should be effectively influenced by the government.

8. **Provision of Finance and Markets:** Governments should provide adequate financial facilities to industries for productivity improvement. Further, government should develop and enlarge national and international markets. The capital markets should be made investment-oriented.

9. **Social and Political Environment:** It is the responsibility of the government to create favourable social and political environment which would promote industrial prosperity. Stable political environment creates confidence among entrepreneurs. And, necessary change in social environment should be brought about in a gradual manner.

10. **Follow-up Action:** Launching of productivity improvement programmes are not enough, government should be alert and should stimulate the entrepreneurs and the workers in maintaining their efforts in this direction.

Gains of Productivity:

Productivity can be increased by adopting the following steps:

1. Worker's participation in management should be encouraged.
2. Mutual trust and cooperation between management and Trade Unions (as collective labour).
3. Introduce rationalisation and automation.
4. Improvement of working conditions and living standard of workers.
5. To make a record of work done and report the same to higher authorities.
6. Provision of training to workers.
7. Reduction of wastage of resources by:
   (a) Establishing control measures;
   (b) Recycling of waste products;
8. Reduction of idle hours and overtime.
9. Uninterrupted supply of raw materials, components etc.
10. Timely maintenance of plant, equipments etc.
11. Introduce simplification in work.
12. Introduce plant layout, machine tools, in such a way that minimum movement is possible.

Productivity Movement in India and Productivity Councils:

- The performance of the Indian economy since the country adopted the process of planned economic development has been very satisfactory. The productivity movement attained significant place in the country's economic growth in the planning period. But, in spite of the large potential of the resources both natural and human – India continues to remain in the group of underdeveloped countries.

- On the eve of the First Five Year Plan, the Indian planners realised that the solution to solve the problem of India's poverty lies in raising the productivity levels. It has been reiterated in the subsequent plans also, that the economy's progress lies in the maximum utilisation of scarce resources.

- On April 1982, the meeting of the National Productivity Council, **Dr. Manmohan Singh** pointed out that though, since Independence, India has made remarkable progress in the industrial and economic fields, the truth remains that growth in the levels of productivity both in agricultural and industrial sector and even in other sectors such as banking, post and telegraph has been low. This is evident from the fact that the capital output ratio has risen from roughly 3:1 in 1950's to 6:1 at present.

- Since 1970's the growth in industrial productivity has been discouraging and almost stagnant though there has been a great amount of investment in the industrial sector throughout the planning period in the country.

- The measures for bringing improvement in productivity need a multidimensional approach that involves suitable changes in social, political, economic and technological aspects. Though it is not known for certain as to how these different variables react upon one another and is also difficult to measure the exactness of impact of each factor on industrial productivity.

- As pointed out earlier, technology has a great impact an industrial productivity. However, in many of our oldest industries such as cotton textiles, sugar, cement etc. Indian management has failed to change the technology and is considered as compared to developed nations. This technological gap between the developed countries and India is viewed in the fall in India's exports in terms of percentage of world exports.

- India's policy of import-substitution followed during 1960-1970 restricted the flow of the latest foreign technology by giving protection to the old indigenous technology from the foreign competition. However, since 1980 there has been liberalisation of import policy and import of the latest technology from developed nations is likely to have a positive impact both on India's technology progress and industrial productivity.

- After discussing technological factor, we now point towards the managerial factor influencing productivity. In India management is still old-fashioned based on hereditary lines. Modern business is an extremely complex one and needs professional experts in all branches- marketing, accounting, financial etc. Thus, India needs professionalisation of management in the place of old-style management. The far-sighted management in India winning the co-operation of workers and adopting modern management techniques can go a long way in raising the industrial productivity.

- Further, worker's participation in management and in decision-making i.e. democratic management would cut down man-days lost due to strikes and lockouts and would add to industrial productivity. Indian management still appears to be autocratic and labour participation schemes have not recorded any great success. This must change if industrial and labour productivity in India are to increase.

- Industrial policy of the Government of India has an adverse impact on industrial productivity.

- The Monopolistic Restrictive Trade Practice (MRTP) Act though well-intentioned resulted in fragmentation of industrial units. The economics of scale and reduction in cost could not be achieved because of various restrictions on the size and output to achieve some social objective such as avoiding concentration of economic power in a few hands of industrial houses.

- With restrictions on the size of industrial units also obstructs the adoption of latest technology for the full utilisation of latest technology needs large scale unit. Thus, it can be said that the MRTP Act has been responsible for technological backwardness by limiting the size of the industrials units.

- Government policy of bringing about industrial dispersal has discouraged industrial agglomeration. And, industrial agglomeration has its own advantages of favourably influencing industrial investment decisions and level of technology to be adopted.

- The Industrial Policy of the Government has to make suitable measures to increase industrial productivity. In this direction, the new economic policy has made a positive movement.

- From the First Five Year Plan, there has been emphasis on raising productivity in the Indian Industries. In 1956 an Indian delegation was sent to Japan to study the constitution and working of the Japanese Productivity Centre. The delegation suggested that a national movement should be started to improve the productivity in the Indian industries. It recommended setting up of an autonomous Indian Productivity Council at the Central Level. On this Council would include representatives from Government, private industrialists, workers and experts from various concerned fields.

- The recommendations took shape in the form of the National Productivity Council in 1958. It is an autonomous body with a maximum of 60 members having equal representation of Government, workers and private industrialists.

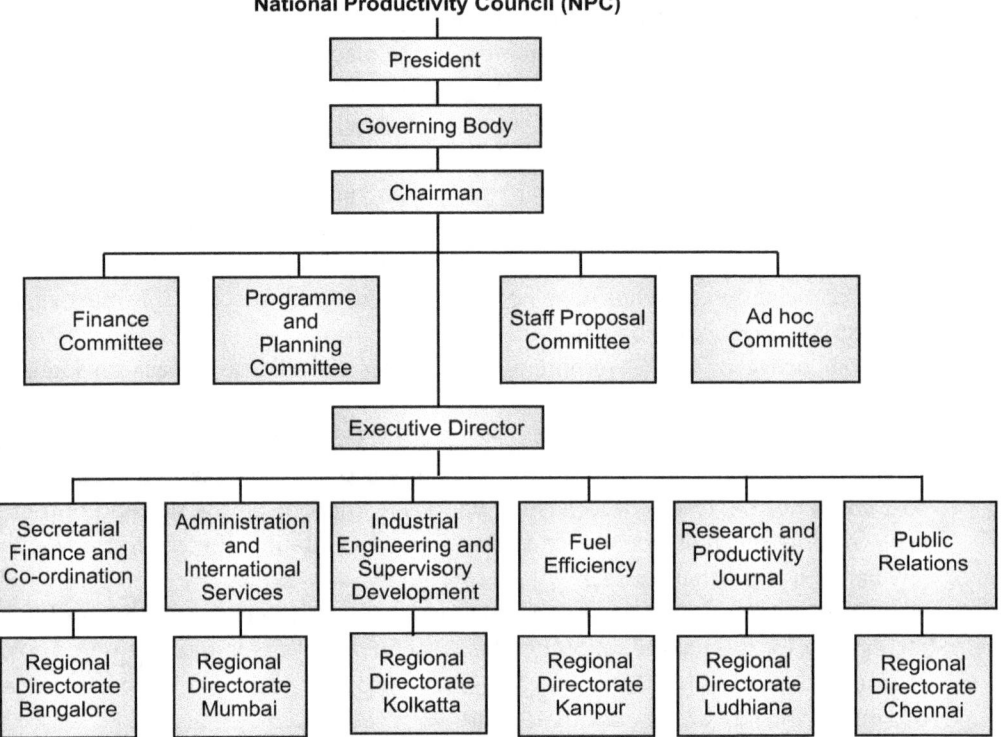

Fig. 3.3: National Productivity Council (NPC)

- An eight-point programme was decided in the first meeting of the National Productivity Council.
- It was decided to make all concerned conscious of the significance of raising the productivity, to provide necessary training facilities and also provide experts to Regional Productivity Councils, promote visits to industrial establishments, conduct research in productivity, visit to developed countries and invite experts from abroad to provide necessary guidance.
- Thus, the NPC was entrusted with the task of stimulating and facilitating the formation of Local Productivity Councils (LPCs). So far 49 LPCs have been established.
- The National Productivity Council has established special bodies in important industries and the Productivity Councils have been doing positive work through serious discussions and by arranging training programmes.

- The year 1966 was declared as "India Productivity Year" to stimulate productivity movement. Top priority was given to organise co-ordination between management, workers and Government and to solve some of the problems facing the country in industrial fields.
- At present the essence of productivity movement in India can be attributed to the achievement of NPC though there are other instruments like Indian Statistical Institute, Indian Institute of Technology, Kharagpur, Tata Institute of Social Sciences, Mumbai etc.
- At present, the unions and managements had several productivity agreements in different organisations. The wages are also linked with productivity in some organisations. Productivity consciousness has been created among the workers and managers. They are being given productivity awards and incentives.
- In the 90's the Indian Economy faced with a formidable challenge to maintain and accelerate the tempo of economic growth, to combat inflation and to meet the ever rising demand of goods and services.
- In recent years, Indian economy is enjoying the advantages of a high saving rate, a large reservoir of skill base and quite a high degree of self reliance in goods and services. And, at this point, productivity can play a pivotal role in achieving goals set-forth for the Ninth Five Year Plan. Every year, several organisations in India have been celebrating 'Productivity Weeks' or 'Productivity Months'. And, during this period, several activities are being taken up to improve productivity at all levels.

To sum up, the productivity movement in India, though attained significant momentum in the right direction, the results are too poor to be adequate to the needs of the country's industrial development. India requires more researchers, more practical men rather than only preachers.

Points to Remember

- **Industrial productivity** is closely linked with Economic Growth and is essential for raising production per unit.
- **Productivity** is a ratio between the total 'output' and the total 'input' of resources used in the process of any economic activity.
- Productivity is influenced by different factors.
- In general, productivity refers more in labour force.
- Different thinkers have defined the term productivity differently, yet the one given by ILO is considered as the most suitable one.
- **Productivity** indicates the magnitude of changes in the economic activity; its scope embraces all the facets of economic welfare.
- **Productivity** is a statistical measure and thus serves as an effective tool of economic analysis.
- **The indices of productivity** serve as indicators of the changes in economic and industrial organisation of the country.

- Though 'Production' and 'Productivity' are closely linked but are different from each other.
- Productivity is a ratio between output and input.
  Symbolically, **Productivity** = Net Output ÷ Effort Input.
  Labour Productivity = Net Output ÷ Number of Workers or Man-Hours.
  Capital Productivity = Net Output ÷ Net Capital Employed.
- There are several limitations in measurement of Productivity.
- **Various Tools of improving productivity are :**
  (i)   By improving industrial relations,
  (ii)   By providing training to workers,
  (iii) By mutual agreement between management and workers,
  (iv)   Scientific management techniques to be used,
  (v)   Work, time and motion studies to be carried out etc.
- **The Determining Factors of Industrial Productivity are :**
  (i)   National Factors,
  (ii)   Technological Factors,
  (iii)   Financial Factors,
  (iv)   Labour Force,
  (v)   Size of the Industry,
  (vi)   Managerial Factors,
  (vii)   Institutional Factors,
  (viii) Government Policies etc.

Questions for Discussion

1. Explain the meaning of Industrial Productivity.
2. Define Industrial Productivity.
3. Discuss the scope and significance of Productivity.
4. Explain the difference between the two terms 'production' and 'productivity'.
5. Write Short Notes on :
    (a) Measurement of Productivity.
    (b) Problems of Productivity Measurement.
6. "Industrial Productivity has its own tools of measurement". Explain this statement.
7. Give detailed information of the factors affecting Industrial Productivity.
8. In brief, explain the misconceptions of productivity.
9. Trace out the productivity movement in India.
10. Write Short Note on: "Productivity Councils'.
11. Discuss the different Indices of Productivity.
12. Explain the role of managerial personnel in improving productivity.
13. How can Government play a positive role for increasing Industrial Productivity?
14. What do you mean by 'Share of Gains in Productivity'?

■■■

Chapter **4**...

Industrial Efficiency and Profitability

Contents ...

Learning Objectives ...

At the end of the Chapter, you will be able:

* To learn about the meaning and definition of industrial efficiency
* To possess knowledge of measurement of industrial efficiency
* To understand the factors affecting industrial efficiency and the measures adopted to improve it
* To be aware of the concept, meaning and measurement of industrial profitability

4.1 Introduction

Industrial efficiency has many dimensions which are to be examined to be well understood. An economic system is economically efficient if it is technically efficient and if it succeeds in rationing out its scarce resources, and the scarce products of these resources in the most desirable way. There are various internal and external forces that determine industrial efficiency.

A simple and widely used index of assessing efficiency of a firm is profitability. Often we find inter-industry and inter-firm differences in profitability and these variations can be attributed to several factors. Certain factors such as market concentration, product diversification, absolute size of a firm, vertical integration, etc., influence profitability of a firm and of an industry.

Further, advertisement, marketing policies, pricing, collusion, and so on i.e., 'market conduct' also affect profitability. With regard to factors such as changes in cost of production, market demand, government policies, etc., influence profitability. When all the possible determinants of profitability are taken into account, its empirical analysis becomes quite complex.

4.2 Meaning and Definition of Industrial Efficiency

The core of any economic activity, whether it is consumption or production, is to strive for maximum possible efficiency. Since the aim of our study is the behaviour of the firm and industries, hence the term 'efficiency' can be understood from the point of view of 'industrial efficiency'.

The term **'Industrial efficiency'** has many dimensions. For instance, a firm, as a technical unit, engaged in production of commodity has a job to transform a set of given inputs into some output which is defined by the production function. In this case, the focus will be on achieving maximum **'productive efficiency'**.

If the firm is defined as an organisational unit which is engaged in production and 'disposal' of a commodity for some desired purpose, then the focus and emphasis will be on achieving **'economic' efficiency'**.

Types of Industrial/Productive Efficiency:

Productive or industrial efficiency has been defined by **Farrell** in terms of two main components:

(i) **Technical efficiency:** This is a purely technical term. It may have anyone of the following forms:
   - It can be a machine or appliance or organisation that is technically efficient if it is adequate to the demands made on it, or lives up to the claims made for it. For example, reliability and quickness of courier in its deliveries.
   - It may mean doing a job in the cheapest possible way, for instance, production of a given level of output with the most optimum combination of inputs.
   - It may mean an assessment of efficiency on the basis of some quantitative standard of performance.

As far as the assessment of efficiency in terms of doing work in cheapest possible way or measuring them in terms of a standard of performance, are linked together, since avoidance of loss or wastage is one way of maximising output from the given set of inputs.

(ii) Factor Price efficiency: It measures the skill in achieving the best combination of the inputs by considering their relative prices. The relative prices are taken into account when one input can be substituted for another in the process of production.

Fig. 4.1 depicts the two types of industrial efficiency. It can be shown with the help of isoquant curve and the budget-line.

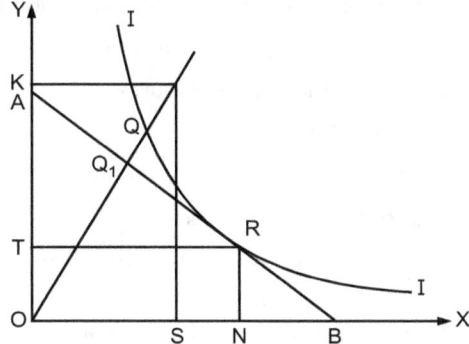

Fig. 4.1: Shows Technical and Productive Efficiency

- **II** is an isoquant which shows the *most efficient* combinations of the two factors X_1 and X_2 used to produce a given output level of a commodity.
- Most efficient combination means the minimum combinations of the factors required according to the 'best practice' production function for the commodity.
- Inefficiency in the factor uses may be a result due to the deviation of a firm from II curve.
- Let us take P as the actual situation where the firm uses OS and OK quantities of the two factors X_1 and X_2 respectively to produce that specific output level.
- The **technical efficiency** of the firm at P in relation to the 'best practice' frontier II can be measured by the ratio OQ/OP.
- **AB** is the iso-cost line indicating the combinations of the two factors that can be purchased from a given amount of money and given factor prices.
- The factor price efficiency for the firm can be measured by the ratio OQ_1/OP. The reason is that any combination of the two factors beyond AB line will not be possible as the quantity of total resources and factor prices are fixed.
- Productive/Industrial efficiency $= \dfrac{OQ}{OP} \times \dfrac{OQ1}{OQ} = \dfrac{OQ1}{OP}$

Higher the productive efficiency when the ratio is near to unity

With the tangency condition in the isoquant analysis satisfied at point R and hence at this point the productive efficiency will be the maximum.

Each firm tries to achieve productive efficiency but it is difficult to achieve since the planning of managers responsible for production may not be perfect, the coordination of the complex operations may be difficult and inadequate, etc.

Productive efficiency in business is only a partial requirement. A broader term is the 'economic efficiency' or the 'business efficiency' from a firm's point of view.

Economic efficiency depends on: (a) resources at the disposal of the firm are scarce; and (b) they have alternative uses. Given the scarce resources and their alternative uses, it is quite natural for a rational firm to get the best from them.

For the entire economic system of a community, 'economic efficiency' implies:

- efficient selection of goods to be produced,
- efficient allocation of resources in the production of these goods,
- efficient choice of the methods of production,
- efficient allotment of the goods produced among the consumers.

It is argued that right application of the economic principles will lead to optimal efficiency in the allocation and utilisation of all resources.

4.3 Measurement of Industrial Efficiency

Measurement means *'quantification'* which is essential in industrial economics to make it empirically relevant.

There is no unique method of measuring industrial efficiency or its components. For example, to measure *technical efficiency* one can measure it through some physical indicators such as capital-output ratio, capital-labour ratio, or actual cost- standard cost ratio, etc.

It is difficult to measure the overall efficiency of a firm, whether productive or economic efficiency.

There are three methods to measure industrial efficiency:

(a) Use of some type of optimisation model such as the linear programming;

(b) Use of the ratios like total productivity or profitability ratios;

(c) Use of econometric methods.

(a) Optimisation Model:

In the first method, a firm has to specify in quantitative terms the objective function and the constraints faced to achieve that and then apply the standard mathematical tools to solve the problem, using simple linear programming problem.

Illustration: The first method is explained with the help of a simple linear programming problem.

A manufacturer is planning to manufacture 2 products by using 3 inputs- labour, machine hours and one raw material.

For one unit of *product A*, it requires one man-hour, one machine-hour and two units of the raw material.

For one unit of *product B*, it requires 3 man-hours, one machine hour, and one unit of raw material.

The total amounts of the inputs are fixed and given as 18 man-hours, 8 machine hours and 14 units of raw material per day.

The price that he expects for the two products in the market and at that price he will be actually able to sell them is ₹ 10 and ₹ 20.

What should be the most efficient level of output of the two products?

Q_1 and Q_2 are the levels of output of the two products: A and B respectively at the optimality situation. The objective of the manufacturer will be to maximise the total sales (i.e. revenue).

The revenue (sales) equation for the manufacturer is:

$$R = 10Q_1 + 20Q_2 \qquad \text{... (i)}$$

To produce Q_1 and Q_2 levels of the outputs, the input demand-supply equations will be:

$$Q_1 + 3Q_2 \leq 18 \qquad \text{... (ii)}$$

$$Q_1 + Q_2 \leq 8 \qquad \text{... (iii)}$$

$$2Q_1 + Q_2 \leq 14 \qquad \text{... (iv)}$$

Each of these equations shows that the utilisation of the input cannot be more than the availability. There is no negative output of either product, i.e.

$$Q_1 \geq 0 \qquad \text{... (v)}$$

$$Q_2 \geq 0 \qquad \text{... (vi)}$$

Now the problem is to maximise total revenue expressed by equation (i) subject to the constraints expressed by equations (ii) to (v).

Graphical representation

Fig. 4.2 depicts the shape obtained by plotting all constraints on a two-dimensional graph.

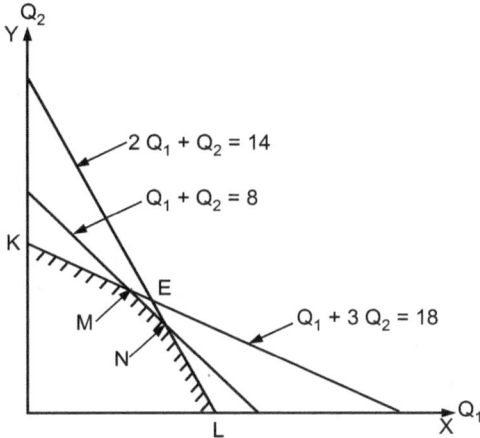

Fig. 4.2: Optimisation: Linear Programming Problem

- The area bounded by all the constraints that is OLNMK is defined as the feasible area from which he combination of Q_1 and Q_2 outputs can be chosen.
- Any point *inside this area* will be feasible but inefficient since resource utilisation will be full.
- Any point *on the boundary* LNMK will be feasible and technically efficient showing full utilisation of at least one input.
- This boundary is the 'Production Possibility Frontier'.
- There will be *only one such point on this boundary* which will be economically most efficient from the manufacturer's point of view, a point where production function is tangent to the boundary.
- We need not draw the tangent but just note down the coordinates (Q_1, Q_2) of these points.
- Substituting the coordinates in the revenue equation, we can get the best one, as shown below in table 4.1.

Table 4.1

Point	Coordinates (Q_1, Q_2)	Revenue (R = $10Q_1 + 20Q_2$)
L	7, 0	₹ 70
N	6, 2	₹ 100
M	3, 5	₹ 130
K	0, 6	₹ 120

- Maximum revenue for the manufacturer is at point M showing 3 units of product A and 5 units of product B.
- This is the point of *maximum economic efficiency* for the manufacturer.
- To conclude,
- The programming methods are ideal for determination of the efficiency conditions but there is a question-mark about their actual uses in the business circles.
- Few large corporations having sophisticated planning machinery may adopt them but in general they adopt their own ad hoc techniques for the efficiency maximisation.
- The choice of the indicators for the efficiency measurement depends on the goals of the firm.

(b) Ratio Method (Use of the Ratios):
- As said above the optimisation model has limited use even in large corporations. The manufacturers will select some performance indicators consistent with their desired intentions in the business.
- Firms may set some target for total factor-productivity or profitability for themselves. If they achieve that one, then they may be called efficient.
- Total factor-productivity is a ratio of the gross revenue divided by the total cost of production.

$$\text{Total factor-productivity} = \frac{\text{Gross Revenue}}{\text{Total Cost of Production}}$$

- Profitability is the return on the capital invested in the business.
- The choice of the indicators for the efficiency or performance measurement depends on the goals and objectives of the firm.

(c) Econometric Method:
- The use of econometric techniques for measuring industrial efficiency is most elegant and scientific in nature.
- Based on economic reasoning, models are specified to measure technical and business efficiencies of the firms and industries separately.
- Quantitative estimation of the parameters and other properties of the models provide fairly reliable estimates of the efficiencies both for the firms and industries.
- However, measuring such efficiencies with the help of the econometric techniques is not an easy task. It requires skills and strong data base.

(d) Production Function:
- The estimation of technical efficiency is normally done by using the production function, the conceptual framework provided by M.J. Farrell (as shown in Fig. 4.2)
- The basic step is to estimate the production possibility frontier underlying a sample of firms in the industry.

- After the frontier is estimated, efficiency of individual units can be measured on the basis of the actual shortfall in output from the estimated frontier.
- Two types of frontiers are used for this purpose: (i) deterministic and (ii) stochastic.
- In a deterministic frontier framework it is assumed that all firms share a common production function which is deterministic and that all variation in firm's performance in respect to it is attributed to variation in firm's efficiencies.

However, this framework ignores the fact that the performance of a firm may be affected by factors outside its control as well as internal factors (in firm's control).

A more realistic approach to estimate technical inefficiency is to use stochastic production function.

It helps to distinguish symmetric and asymmetric disturbances bearing upon a production plan.

In other words, it is assumed that production possibilities vary randomly from firm to firm in response to exogenous (external) factors unrelated to technical inefficiency and so that they operate on or beneath their stochastic production possibility frontiers.

Thus the maximum productive capacity of a firm is determined partly by the technology and resources under its control (internal forces) and partly by the environment within which it operates and over which it has no control (exogenous factors).

A number of economists suggest the approach of using stochastic production frontiers.

Business Efficiency: Another important aspect of industrial efficiency is business efficiency or economic efficiency. Its measurement by using econometric techniques is as complex as that of the technical efficiency.

It is based on a relationship between the performance variable like profit rate and its determinants.

Depending upon the goals of the objectives of the firm the performance variable is carefully to be chosen and then through valid economic arguments the determinants are to be identified. Among the determinants one has to include market structural variables, managerial and organisational variables, several qualitative variables affecting the performance of the firm.

However, selection of all such variables is not easy, but once the variables are picked up, then estimation of their impact on the performance of the firm can be done by using multiple regression frameworks.

4.4 Factors Affecting Industrial Efficiency

For simplicity purpose, the factors or determinants influencing industrial efficiency can be grouped into two categories:

(i) Internal forces;
(ii) External forces.

Internal Forces

In this category we include all those activities which define the *managerial function of a firm.*

For economic efficiency one must have -

- efficient planning and regulation of the operations;
- a willingness to accept changes in the policies related to the conduct of the business;
- technological innovations;
- a smooth flow of work;
- proper supervision;
- adequate facilities for work including fair play, etc.

The above activities are the work of the management. The management is responsible for making proper policies and to execute them.

Any inefficiency on the part of the management will make the entire operations inefficient, resulting in low economic or industrial efficiency.

The Managerial or organisational slackness (or 'internal inefficiency') is a mixture of all internal forces causing economic inefficiency in business.

External Forces

1. **Market Structure:** It includes the number and size distribution of the firms in the industry; the number and size distribution of the buyers in the market for the products of the industry; the number of competing products; the conditions of entry in the industry, etc. If the market is very much competitive for the firm, then the inefficiency may be very low or not at all in this situation. It is because the inefficient factor or product will be thrown out of the industry due to the strong competition.

   On the other hand, if there is monopoly (single firm in the industry), then it will not be subjected to market competition. This may result in poor performance of the firm and may use its resources inefficiently. Whatever may be the situation, it is a strong proposition that the market structure exerts a great influence on the performance or efficiency of a firm.

2. **Power Breakdown:** If there is power break-down, production will be affected adversely, sales or profits will decline and so the efficiency of the firm will be poor.

3. **Market Imperfection:** All external forces together may create conditions for the market imperfection which eventually influence the 'allocative efficiency' of the firm.

   The 'allocative efficiency' is defined through a set of general equilibrium conditions.

   It occurs when output is at that level where marginal cost equals price in each product for each firm.

   The 'allocative efficiency' has important implications on the economic efficiency of the firm from the social point of view.

4. **Labour:** Human resource has a great impact on industrial efficiency. Skilled, literate human resource leads to promotion of industrialisation and industrial efficiency.

5. **Technical Know-how:** Progress in technical know-how gives a break-through in combinations of inputs and the resultant output. Efficient technology leads to positive outcome in efficiency of manufacturing units. Technology extends the production frontier of an industry. Thus, the application of technology in manufacturing processes results in higher efficiency, greater degree of specialisation.

6. **Government Regulations:** Competition creates conditions for a firm to strive towards efficiency and maximise profits. On the other hand, protection tends to make the firm complacent and inefficient in the long-run. Thus, the policy of the government for firms – to provide protection or not- determines the industrial efficiency in firms in external sector. Further, the tariffs, taxes levied, etc., determine the industrial efficiency.

7. **Institutional Factors (or Non-economic Factors):** Sociological and cultural factors play a significant role in affecting industrial efficiency. Only when the economic and social institutions are conducive to improvements, will the industrial efficiency improve. A society ridden with caste system hampers horizontal and vertical mobility of labour, thus adversely influencing the productive efficiency. A positive industrial culture, such as desire to work hard, motivated workers, skilled labour, etc., can work towards increasing the industrial efficiency.

8. **Other Factors:** The organisational or structural conditions prevailing in the industry to which the firm belongs, short-term fluctuations in the market for both inputs and output of the firm, trade union activities and government regulations, etc.

To conclude, a review of the factors-internal and external- affecting the economic efficiency of a firm is a difficult task. The present theory of the firm provides only few guidelines for this. The major information on this aspect comes from the empirical analysis of the economic forces operating at the firm and industry levels.

4.5 Measures Adopted by Indian Government, Industries and other Agencies to Improve Industrial Efficiency

Industrial efficiency can be viewed in economic decisions:

- In the free market mechanism, the responsibility of making efficient decisions lies on the prices prevailing in the economy. The price system will be automatically in operation to solve the basic problems of the society and the whole economy will be at the maximum efficiency.

- In the central planning method all major decisions about consumption, production and distribution are taken by the Government with or without use of money prices. The decisions will be administrative in nature.

- To improve labour efficiency it is essential that:
  (a) Minimum wages should be given to the workers to provide for his family a reasonable level of subsistence. A wage structure should be based on sound incentive schemes.
  (b) Employees are stimulated to work enthusiastically when he has an opportunity to grow through adequate promotion.
  (c) Working and living conditions should be good which encourages the worker to contribute more effectively.
  (d) Adequate training would improve the worker's efficiency and in turn the industrial efficiency.
  (e) Security plays an important role in efficiency of labour. A regular and steady job results in better performance by him in the manufacturing unit.
  (f) Suitable laws and legislations that protect the interest of the workers will be healthy to the productive efficiency.
  (g) Training in upgraded and sophisticated technology would improve the technical efficiency.
  (h) Joint Management Councils have been introduced by the Government and workers should be given a chance to participate in the management.
  (i) It is necessary to further liberalise the rules and practices of banking and other financial institutions supplying credit to small-scale industries so that they can arrange adequate credit required for the purpose.
  (j) The government should take measures in lowering the rates of duty and provide export incentives to small entrepreneurs.
  (k) Recognising the significance of small and medium enterprises in terms of their contribution to country's industrial production, exports, employment and creation of industrial base, the Central and State Governments are undertaking several policy measures and incentives and implementing schemes and programmes for promotion and development of these enterprises. The Entrepreneurship Development Programmes (EDPs) aim to create new entrepreneurs by cultivating their latent qualities of entrepreneurship.
  (l) To bridge the gap between the aspirations of the potential entrepreneurs there is a need to support and nurture the potential first generation entrepreneurs by giving then handholding support during the initial stages of setting up and managing their enterprises.
  (m) The progressive de-reservation of products in the MSMEs aimed at providing opportunities for technological upgradation, promotion of exports and economies of scale, with a view to encourage modernisation and enhance competitiveness in the sector.

To conclude, industrial efficiency includes technical and productive efficiency. The efforts of the government, agencies or industries is to secure industrial efficiency by improving technical (by modernisation) and productive efficiency – by diversification, from large scale to small and medium enterprises that have used less capital, creates more employment opportunities.

4.6 Industrial Profitability

Introduction

Profitability is a widely used and simple index of assessing business efficiency of a firm. Inter-industry and inter-firm differences are witnessed in profitability. These differences can be attributed to several factors. Some of the factors, such as market concentration, product diversification, vertical integration, etc., constitute the elements of 'market structure' which affect profitability of a firm and of an industry.

On the other hand, there are factors which constitute elements of 'market conduct' of the firm such as R&D, marketing policies, advertisement, etc., which influence profitability to a great extent. Profitability will also be affected by external constraints such as changes in the cost of production, market demand, government policies, etc.

4.6.1 Meaning of Profitability

Profit is usually interpreted as the difference between the total expenditure involved in making or buying of a commodity and the total revenue accruing from its sales. That is, *profit is difference between total revenue and total expenditure.*

Profitability may also be expressed as the proportion by which the price per unit sold would be greater than the average of marginal cost. This is a rate on turnover which is called 'price-cost margin'.

Both these approaches to conceive the term profitability are not free from ambiguity.

The major difficulty lies with the definition of the term 'profit' itself. Among economists there is no common agreement about the definition and conditions for occurrence of profit.

- Some economists treat profit as an *implicit return* to any service(s) and/or resource(s) supplied by the owner(s) himself. For his personal services in his own business an entrepreneur is supposed to get implicit wage, for the money he puts in he gets implicit interest. All such payments the accountants put under the heading of profit but economists treat them as elements of cost in business.

- F. B. Hawley and other economists treat profit as a reward for risks and responsibilities that the entrepreneur puts himself to. Risks, faced by entrepreneur, are of different kinds. These risks may be associated with holding of the assets, some with stocks of materials and finished goods, technological changes, trade cycle, marketing, etc.

Some of these risks are predictable, i.e., can be anticipated in advance and such risks are insurable. However, in general, there are majority of risks in business which are not predictable or cannot be anticipated in advance and such risks cannot be insured. In such cases, entrepreneur is justified a reward in the form of profit.

- Prof. Knight links the occurrence of profit as a reward for bearing uncertainties rather than the risks which are known in advance and are insurable. Thus, there is another group of risks which arise as a result of future uncertainties.
- Schumpeter sees the origin of profit as a reward to the entrepreneur for the services of innovation. 'Dynamic theory of profit', a theory propounded by J. B. Clark believed profit as reward to changes and dynamic element in business. Economists like Joel Dean and Peter Drucker have given theory on similar lines, i.e., profit to entrepreneur as a reward for innovations.
- The strongest case for occurrence of profit is attributed to the monopoly power. Certain conditions like uneven size distribution of the firms in industries, barriers to entry, economies of scale, product diversification, advertisement, patent rights, etc., together make market structure of the industry imperfect as a result of which some firms having greater share in the industry will be able to control prices and market supply in a way to get maximum surplus.
- Monopoly is the extreme case where we can expect maximum profits. Next in order which can have occurrence of surplus profits are concentrated markets having either 'homogeneous' or 'differentiated' oligopolistic structures. From economist's point of view under perfect competition, there will be no scope for surplus profit, except in short-run.
- To conclude, the source of profit can be implicit earnings of the entrepreneur, and/or reward for risks, uncertainties, and innovations, a return due to monopoly power of the firm.

4.6.2 Factors Determining Profitability

- For long-term profitability, the consideration of growth of the firm assumes prime importance. This requires an adequate and regular supply of capital from within the system. Greater the availability of internal finance, lesser will be dependence on external finance, which is quite crucial particularly in a state of depression in the market.
- Since in a dynamic society the main strength of the firm is innovation, the firm must have an effective research and development so as to update the production technology as well as the product line.
- The general business conditions significantly influence the profitability of a firm. During the conditions of boom all firms make excess profits, while during recession firms make very low profits or even run in losses.

- In short-run, the sales promotion effort, advertising, etc., result in expanding the market for the products, thus resulting in large size of profit. But in the long run their impact is nullified to a great extent by the counter-selling efforts of the competitors.
- The age of the product is vital to influence the demand for the product. For instance, if the product is in the growth stage it will give an optimistic outlook to the demand of the product, while if the product has passed the maturity stage demand for this product will obviously decline and thus affecting the profitability of the company adversely.
- The size of profits is inversely related to the degree of competition. In a monopoly situation, profits will be maximum, and as competition become more intense, the volume of profit will be smaller and smaller.
- The dynamic forces like tastes and preferences of people too determine the profitability of a firm.

4.6.3 Measurement of Industrial Profitability

Profit is an essential reward from the business point of view. As Dean Joel remarked, *"a business firm is an organisation designed to make profit, and profit is the primary measure of its success"*. Even if the firm keeps any other goal than the profit maximisation, yet a firm needs profit for survival, satisfaction, stability and growth.

However, due to the ambiguity about the definition of profit, the argument arises in its measurement. The argument is whether the definition adopted by the accountants is to be followed or the one given by economists.

Other controversies about the definition of profit are- whether it should be *gross or net of interest and taxes,* and whether it is the *short-term profit or the long-term profit* with which the business firms are concerned.

Net Income and Gross Income Margin:

Net income margin is the ratio of net income to sales. Gross profit margin is the ratio of gross profit to sales.

In Accounting terms: As far as measuring profit from accounting sense we find a discrepancy in the **size of the firm**. In case of a small firm which is managed by a proprietor himself the implicit costs will be part of his profit but for large corporations where ownership and management are separate, there may not be any implicit costs and in such a situation the concept of profit equals with the one given by economists.

Let's begin to understand the measurement of profitability with the help of certain key terms.

Profit Margin:	It is the profit made as a proportion of sales revenue.
Gross Profit:	This is calculated by subtracting only variable costs from sales revenue, ignoring fixed costs.
	Thus, Goss Profit = Sales Revenue – Variable Costs.
Net Profit:	This is calculated by subtracting total costs from sales revenue.
	Thus, Net Profit = Sales Revenue – Total Costs.

The profitability of an industry is the average profitability of the companies in that industry. Financially healthy industry sectors have high profitability.

- Profitability is a key metric in business as companies need to know how much they make from their activities.
- Profitability is both an internal metric and a benchmark. High profits often indicate a strong ability of the company to reinvest earnings and compete heavily for its share in the market.

One way to determine profitability is to calculate the ratio of profits to other financial metrics, such as sales, assets or equity.

Each method is proper for measuring financial returns, although a company can only use one it desires.

(a) The Income Statement:

- It represents all sales revenues, cost of goods sold and expenses for a stated time period.
- The Income Statement is part of standard accounting procedures and is usually a monthly report.
- There are two measures of profitability there, with both being important. The first one is Gross Profit – *which is sales revenue less cost of goods sold* and represents the amount of money left after prying for the costs related to inventory sold.
- Net income is gross profit less expenses and it is the money left for reinvesting into the business.

(b) Gross Profit Ratios:

- These ratios are similar profitability measure when compared to the first metric from the income statement.
- However, the formula is *Sales revenue less cost of goods divided by sales revenue.*
- This metric works best for determining the profitability on individual products or product lines and also the overall gross profit ratio.
- It indicates what percent of every rupee goes to pay for inventory costs.
- Firms can use this measure to compare itself against other businesses in the industry.

(c) Debt-Equity Ratio:

There is ambiguity even when treating of interest on loan capital in profit accounting.

- If actual interest payments have been deducted before the calculation of profit, then comparison of profit between firms will be affected by their **debt-equity ratio or gearing ratio.**
- But, if interest is not deducted, then the comparison of profit will be affected by the inter-firm differences in capital intensity.

(d) Depreciation Accounting:

- Provisions of depreciation and taxes create serious conceptual and measurement problems in profit analysis as they are likely to vary from firm to firm depending on the method adopted for estimation and taxation laws respectively.
- For example, a large firm may follow different method for depreciation accounting than a smaller one. Further, it may pay higher rate of tax than the smaller firm, so the profits of such firms will not be comparable directly.

(e) Return on Investment/ Return on Capital:
- Another way of measuring the profitability of a business or a new business project is to compare the profit made with the value of the capital invested. This gives the return on capital.
- The higher the result of this ratio, the more profitable the investment has been and it could also indicate the efficiency of the management in managing the investment.
- Thus, 'Return on capital' is the proportion that the 'net profit' is of the capital invested in the business or project.

$$\text{Return on Capital (\%)} = \frac{\text{Net Profit}}{\text{Capital Invested}} \times 100$$

- It is a measurement that reviews the profitability for various projects in which a company engages.

(f) Hybrid Profit Metric:

Hybrid profit metrics or other profit measures may be more appropriate for a company. These may include time value of money measurements, the statement of cash flows, or return on equity ratios.

The total amount of profit, whatever is its definition or measuring procedure, is of little value unless it is related to the scale of business firm in which it is generated. For this reason, *the profitability of a business is generally defined in terms of a profit rate which expresses total profit as a percentage of either total assets or sales.*

What should be the denominator to compute profit rate depends upon the objective with which it is being measured. For example, a shareholder will be interested in the relationship between net profit and nominal value of share capital; a salaried manager may be interested with effective utilisation of all resources and as such he may compute profit rates using sales or total cost of production as denominator.

Both sales and total cost of production are annual flows. The profit rates obtained by using them as denominator will give us a short-term perspective of profitability. The return on total assets will provide us long-term perspective of profitability.

The common measures of profit rates are as follows:

	Gross	Net
Return on Capital (long-term profitability)	$\dfrac{R-D}{K}$	$\dfrac{R-C}{K}$
Price-Cost Margin (short-term profitability).	$\dfrac{R-D}{R}$	$\dfrac{R-C}{R}$

Where,

R = Total revenue;

D = Total direct cost;

C = Total cost of production;

K = Total assets.

To include corporate tax on profits, the above rates can be modified. The net profitability with respect to assets (K) would now be, $(1 - t) \dfrac{R - C}{K}$ and with respect to sales $(1 - t) \dfrac{R - C}{R}$, where t = corporate tax rates.

To conclude, there is really no end to the methods available when measuring profit. The company must simply assess the formula against the need and select the appropriate profitability measure.

We can increase profit by:

1. Increasing Total Revenue
2. Decreasing Total Costs.

Thus, **Methods of Increasing Profit:**

*   Increase sales without reducing the net profit margin.
*   Increase net profit by reducing variable costs per unit.
*   Increase net profit margin by increasing price.
*   Increase net profit margin by reducing fixed costs.

Problems in Computation of Profitability:

Let us understand the problems in conceptualisation and measurement of profit with the following illustration:

$$P = R - C$$

Where,   P = Profit;

                R = Revenue; and

                C = Total cost of production

Now, P is gross or net profit depends on what is included in C.

$$C = rK + D$$

where   K = Capital stock in value terms,

                r = rate of return covering depreciation, interest and risk premium appropriate to the industry

                D = direct cost such as labour cost, material cost, fuel and power, selling costs, managerial remuneration, etc.

                R = total revenue or income that accrues to the firm.

R includes 3 components, viz., value of products and by-products, changes in the value of stocks of finished goods, and other income such as equipment sold by the firm, work done for consumer, etc.

In measurement of profitability regarding R there is not much ambiguity except for some problem in valuation of inventories of goods, recovery of capital invested, etc.

The problem that appears in measurement is on the cost side.

First we take direct cost (D): It includes all items of costs, implicit or explicit, except depreciation and imputed interest which are accounted by rK.

- While computing D accountants ignore implicit cost items but economists include them. For large firms management and ownership functions are separate and hence there will be no implicit costs of entrepreneurship but in small firms entrepreneurs do perform management functions and employ their self-owned resources in business for which they get implicit returns. Thus, the problem arises as to what should be the criteria for such payments? If payments are included in D they are likely to cause a bias as the entrepreneurs may have high cost for their services. To avoid such bias accountants are right in excluding them from D but economically it cannot be excluded.

'Goodwill' (intangible asset): There is also a doubt about inclusion of selling and advertisement expenditure in Direct costs (D).

- By advertisement expenditure and costs a stock of 'goodwill' is created in the market for the firm's products. 'Goodwill' is intangible asset and any expenditure to increase the stock of 'goodwill' should be interpreted as capital expenditure and not as a component in D (i.e. direct cost).
- Only the depreciation, imputed interest and risk premium on advertisement capital expenditure should be included in the direct cost.
- However, in practice advertisement and selling expenses are treated as annual cost items and are included in the cost for profit measurement.

Element K and r: There are difficulties in measurement of stock of capital K and the rate of r.

- There is no satisfactory measurement for K. Accountants express as historical cost but economists argue for replacement cost as a true measure for K.
- The replacement cost is difficult to assess precisely as it is difficult to find their current costs of assets and there will be no second hand markets in which their opportunity costs may be evaluated.
- Further, another dispute issue is to take gross value or net value of K. From accounting side the net value makes a sense but in common practice the gross value of K is used.

Depreciation: The rate of depreciation is a major component of r has no unique value. It depends on the method of depreciation accounting chosen by the firm such as straight line depreciation method, declining balance method, etc.

Risk margin: The coverage of risk margin is also difficult to find as there are no set methods for it. In this case subjective judgements play a dominant role while assessing the riskiness of a business.

Conclusion: The concept of profit is very much ambiguous and hence there are problems in its measurement. Such problems will have their impact on measurement of the profitability of a firm.

Points to Remember

- The term 'Industrial efficiency' has many dimensions. For instance, a firm, as a technical unit, engaged in production of commodity has a job to transform a set of given inputs into some output which is defined by the production function. In this case, the focus will be on achieving maximum 'productive efficiency'.
- If the firm is defined as an organisational unit which is engaged in production and 'disposal' of a commodity for some desired purpose, then the focus and emphasis will be on achieving 'economic' efficiency.
- Technical efficiency
- Factor Price efficiency.

Factors Affecting Industrial Efficiency: The factors or determinants influencing industrial efficiency can be grouped in two categories:

- **Internal Forces:** In this category we include all those activities which define the *managerial function of a firm.*
  For economic efficiency one must have -
  o efficient planning and regulation of the operations;
  o a willingness to accept changes in the policies related to the conduct of the business;
  o technological innovations;
  o a smooth flow of work;
  o proper supervision;
  o adequate facilities for work including fair play, etc.
- **External Forces:**
  o Market Structure ;
  o Power breakdown;
  o Market Imperfection;
  o Labour;
  o Technical Know-how;
  o Government regulations;
  o Institutional Factors (or non-economic factors);
  o Other factors.
- **Methods of measuring Industrial Efficiency:**
  o Econometric Model;
  o Optimisation Model;
  o Ratio Method;
  o Production Function.
- **Meaning of Profitability:** Profit is usually interpreted as the difference between the total expenditure involved in making or buying of a commodity and the total revenue accruing from its sales. That is, *profit is difference between total revenue and total expenditure.*

- **Methods of Measuring Profitability:**
  - o **The Income Statement:** It represents all sales revenues, cost of goods sold and expenses for a stated time period.
  - o **Gross Profit Ratios:** Sales revenue less cost of goods divided by sales revenue.
  - o **Debt-Equity Ratio** treating of interest on loan capital in profit accounting.
  - o **Return on Investment/Return on Capital:** To compare the profit made with the value of the capital invested. This gives the return on capital.
  - o **Hybrid Profit Metric:** These may include time value of money measurements, the statement of cash flows, or return on equity ratios.
  - o **Common Measure:** Both sales and total costs of production are annual flows. The profit rates obtained by using them as denominator will give us a short-term perspective of profitability. The return on total assets will provide us long-term perspective of profitability.

- **Problems in Measurement of Profitability are related to:**
  - o Direct cost (D)
  - o 'Goodwill'
  - o Element K and r
  - o Depreciation
  - o Risk margin

Questions for Discussion

1. Define 'Industrial efficiency'.
2. What do you mean by 'industrial efficiency'?
3. Discuss the various factors that affect 'industrial efficiency'.
4. Write in detail the various methods of measuring 'industrial efficiency'.
5. Explain and define the term 'profitability'.
6. Discuss the methods of measuring profitability.
7. What problems are faced while computing profitability of any company or a firm?
8. Describe the various factors that influence profitability.
9. What do you mean by profitability?
10. Write a short note on the internal and external forces that influence industrial efficiency.

■■■

Chapter **5**...

Industrial Profile and Problems

Contents ...

5.1   Introduction
5.2   Industrial Profile
5.3   Structure and Organisation of Large Scale Industries in India
5.4   Private Sector Enterprises: Role, Functions and Problems
5.5   Public Sector Enterprises: Role, Functions and Problems
5.6   Disinvestment Policies
5.7   Micro, Small and Medium Enterprises (MSMEs): Role and Problems
 ➢   Points to Remember
 ➢   Questions for Discussion

Learning Objectives ...

At the end of the Chapter, you will be able:
 •   To learn about the Structure and Organisations of Large Scale Industries
 •   To know about the Public Sector Enterprises, their Role, Functions and Problems
 •   To know the Disinvestment Policies
 •   To know about the Micro, Small and Medium Enterprises, their Role and Problems

5.1 Introduction

Business activity creates goods and services. A business is a combination of industrial and commercial activities i.e. production and distribution of goods and services.

Such business activities in India are carried through many of the following arrangements based on ownership and management:

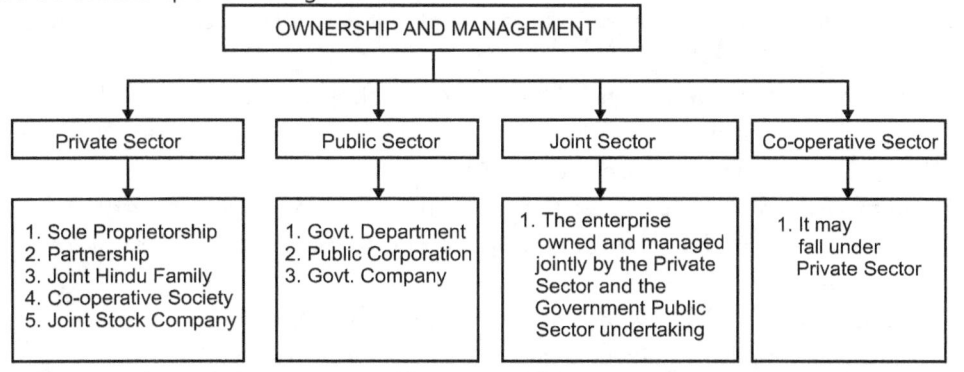

OR ON THE BASIS OF ECONOMIC IDEOLOGY

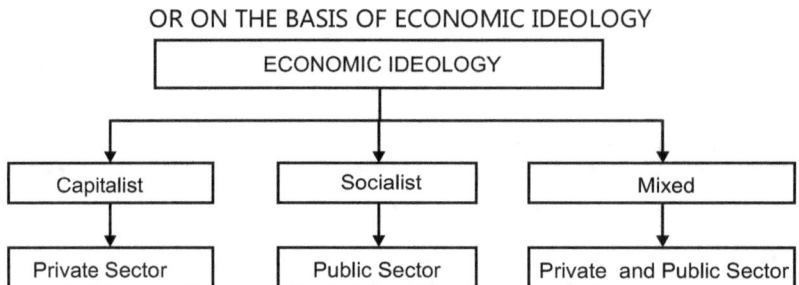

- **A Capitalist Economy (or laissez faire):** It encourages privately owned and managed business. There is no interference of the Government in economic business.
- **A Socialist (or Communist) Economy:** In such an economy, economic activities are owned by the State or the nation, i.e. production, distribution etc. is concentrated in public sector.
- **A Pure Capitalist or Socialist:** These forms are theoretical, while a mixed economy is the practice of the day (a mix of public and private sector) e.g. India.

In private sector, the ownership and management are in the hands of private individuals. That is, they have freedom to decide and act within the framework of the national policies e.g. economic, fiscal, industrial licensing etc.

Classification of Industries

Industries may thus be classified on following basis:

(A) Ownership:

An enterprise may be wholly owned by the government, wholly owned by a private individual or group of individuals or jointly owned by the government and the private groups.

1. **Public Sector Enterprises:** When all enterprises are owned wholly by the government. Government, here includes Central, State or Local Government. For example, Indian Airlines Corporation, Bharat Heavy Electricals Limited, Rashtriya Ispat Nigam etc.

2. **Private Sector Enterprises:** When all enterprises are wholly owned by private individuals or a group of individuals. For example, Bajaj Auto Limited, Nestle Indian Limited, Hindustan Lever Limited, and Reliance Group of Industries etc.

3. **Joint Ownership Enterprises:** There may be enterprises which are partly owned by the government and partly owned by the private sector. Such enterprise can be of two types.

   (i) Owned jointly by government and foreign company, and

   (ii) Owned jointly by government and country's private sector.

(B) Scale of Production:

Scale implies the size of an enterprise. The size is measured either in terms of capital or number of workers employed. On the basis of scale, industries may be classified into small scale and large scale enterprises.

(C) Use-based Classification:

Goods are used either for consumption or for production. Accordingly industries are classified into consumer goods and producer goods industries.

   (i) Consumer Goods Industries: These units produce goods for consumption e.g. washing machines, watches, clothes etc.

   (ii) Producers Goods Industries: These units produce goods needed for further production e.g. fertilizers, iron and steel, cement, tools etc.

India started her quest for industrial development after independence in 1947. The Industrial Policy Resolution of 1948 marked the beginning of evolution of the Indian Industrial Policy. The Industrial Policy Resolution of 1956 gave the public sector strategic role in the economy. Earmarking the pre-eminent position of the public sector, it envisaged private sector co-existing with the State.

The Industrial Policy initiatives undertaken by the Government of India since July 1991 have been designed to build on the past industrial achievements and to accelerate the process of making Indian industry internationally competitive.

Major policy changes were therefore, introduced in 1991 to provide competitive stimulus for accelerated economic growth. The New Industrial Policy (NIP) has introduced a substantial programme of deregulation. The number of industries reserved for the public sector was reduced to eight. And, even in these, where security and strategic concerns pre-dominate areas private sector participation can be invited on a discretionary basis.

Thus, the NIP opened the ways to private sector and introduced liberalisation, globalisation and privatisation.

5.2 Industrial Profile

Importance of Industries in India Economy: Industries have a very important role to play in our economy due to the following reasons:

1. **Industries produce goods for consumption** to fulfil different needs of consumers. Manufactured goods such as pins, paper, soaps, cycles, sewing machines, refrigerator etc.

2. **Industries produce goods for production units** like for factories, farms, shops, offices etc. e.g. tractors, harvesters, diesel etc. for agriculture sector. Industries need machines; raw materials etc. are produced by industries.

3. **Industries help in the production of services** like producing buses, trucks, trains, instruments for medical services and for communication sector.

4. **Industries help to make us self-reliant** by manufacturing goods like steel, oil etc.
5. **Industries promote exports** and make available the foreign exchange much needed for paying for our imports.
6. **Industries are a source of livelihood** to a number of people in the economy. Industries are an increasing source of employment as compared to agriculture.
7. **Industries help in exploiting natural resources** like mineral deposits, forests, rivers, sea etc. Industrial goods like machines, equipments etc. help in exploiting the existing resources.

For example, for exploiting oil in the sea we require sophisticated machines, satellites and other instruments.

Factors affecting Industrial Growth:

1. Availability of raw materials.
2. Availability of technology.
3. Availability of Infrastructural facilities.
4. Availability of manpower.
5. Employer and employee relations.
6. Demand for goods.

5.3 Structure and Organisation of Large Scale Industries in India

Large-scale industries refer to those industries which require huge infrastructure, man-power and have influx of capital assets.

The term 'large-scale industry' is a generic one including various types of industries in its purview. All the heavy industries in India like iron and steel industry, textile industry, automobile manufacturing industry, fall under the large-scale industrial arena.

However, in recent years, due to the Information Technology (I.T.) boom and the huge amount of revenue generated by it, the I.T. industry can also be included within the jurisdiction of large-scale industrial sector. Last but not the least; the telecom industry also forms an indispensable component of the large-scale industrial sector of India.

Every country needs exploring of coal, iron and steel, exploring of oil and its purification, heavy machineries, heavy electrical equipments, heavy chemicals, ships and aeroplanes, industries of heavy and basic industries for its development. All these industries help to develop agriculture, transport, communication facilities and other industries. It means development of large scale industries is almost essential for the development of heavy and basic industries.

Indian economy is heavily dependent on these large industries for its economic growth, generation of foreign currency and for providing job opportunities to millions of Indians.

Iron and steel forms the indispensable part of the large-scale industrial sector. The iron and steel industry had played a key role in the industrial development of India from the pre-independence period. It also informs us that India has seven large integrated iron and steel plants of which six are owned by the public sector Steel Authority of India (SAIL) and one by the Private sector – Tata Iron and Steel Company Limited- popularly known as TISCO.

Telecom industry is another key player in the large-scale industrial sector of India. This telecom industry has undergone stupendous growth in recent few years and is now posed to be a stalwart of the Indian industrial arena. A major contributor towards the growth of the telecom industry in India is the Association of Unified Telecom Service Providers of India (AUSPI). By the help of their performance in India, the AUSPI members are also helping to shape the future of CDMA technology evolution. They advocate that India can and ought to take a leadership role in defining the future evolution of CDMA.

Another big league player of the large-scale industrial sector of India is the Bio-I.T. or the Pharmaceutical industry of India. Scientific advancement in discovery of drugs and advanced researches has propelled forward Indian Bio-I.T. or pharmaceutical industry.

Textile industry is one of the most formidable pillars of the large-scale industrial structure of India. Indian textile industry like iron and steel industry has done a huge contribution in the overall economic growth of India.

Importance and Functions of Large-Scale Industries

(a) Improvement in Productivity:

In large scale industries work is distributed among the labourers according to their efficiency which improves the productivity. These industries also use huge modern capital which raises productivity and reduces cost per head. It enables the consumer to get commodities at a cheaper rate.

(b) Import Substitution:

Capital goods and consumer goods which are imported from the foreign countries can be produced inside the country through large scale industries. Our country will depend upon foreign countries on heavy chemicals, heavy electricity, chemical fertilizers and other consumer goods, unless we develop large scale industries. Due to the development of large scale industries, all these commodities are produced inside the country and there is no need of import which is known as import substitution.

(c) Export Promotion:

Large scale industries change the pattern of export. Earlier the export items included leather, tea, jute, jute products, spices of different types, and cotton clothes to foreign countries. Due to the development of large scale industries, the country is able to export engineering products, heavy electric products and other industrial products. Thus the composition and quantum of export items have changed due to the large scale industries.

(d) Development of Agricultural Sector:

The development of agricultural sector depends upon the development of large-scale industries. The surplus today witnessed in agricultural sector is due to the machinery, equipment, fertilizers, insecticides, pesticides, etc., supplied by the large-scale industries.

(e) Development of an Economy:

Large-scale industries have a major role to play in the economic development of the underdeveloped countries. The large-scale industries prove as a 'big-push' to the development of an economy.

(f) Providing an Economic Base:

The capital-goods industries, infrastructure, social and basic industries are some of the large scale industries that are essential for the rapid growth of an economy as these industries provide an industrial base to an economy.

(g) It provides Mass Production:

Large-scale industries enable goods to be produced on a mass scale and at reduced cost. These industries have made possible the goods within the reach of masses.

(h) It raises the Standard of Living:

Large-scale industries have helped in raising the standard of living of the masses by providing them goods of latest quality and technology.

(i) It contributes in GNP:

Large-scale industries contribute substantially to the gross national product of the country. These industries have generated sufficient growth in the economy.

(j) Increased Productive Capacity:

Rapid expansion of large scale sector has increased the productive capacity of the industrial sector. A large infra-structure has been built to sustain this sub-continental economy- a network of irrigation, storage works and canals, hydro and thermal power generation, regional power grids, a largely electrified and dieselised railways system, national and state highways on which a rapidly growing road transport fleet can operate and telecommunications system covering most urban centres and linking India with the world.

(k) Large-scale Industries-Public Sector:

Indian economy is a mixed economy and hence private and public sector. To protect the interest of the nation the large-scale industries were mainly public sector. The growth of public sector was in heavy and basic industries, the machine goods sector, engineering industries etc., which provided the industrial base of the economy and thus created basic infrastructure of the economy to enable the private sector to flourish later. Thus, large-scale industries in public sector proved as an engine of growth.

5.4 Private Sector Enterprises: Role, Functions and Problems

Definition and Meaning

The part of the economy that is not state controlled, and is run by individuals and companies for profit. The private sector encompasses all 'for-profit' businesses that are not owned or operated by the government.

The part of national economy made up of private enterprises includes the personal sector (i.e. households) and corporate sector (i.e. companies) and is responsible for allocating most of the resources within an economy.

Objectives of Private Sector

A Private Sector has three major objectives:

1. **The Economic Objective:** This is related to earning of profits, providing goods and services, creation of market, research and development etc.

2. **The Social Objective:** It aims at creation of employment opportunities, supply of quality goods at reasonable price, timely payment of fair wages, proper treatment of workers, providing social welfare facilities etc.

3. **The Socio-Economic Objective:** It includes at satisfying the aim of profit-maximisation and creating capital for future generations without exploiting the environment, labour or consumers.

Role and Function of the Private Sector

1. **Importance for Development:** Schumpeter characterised private sector as the initiator and moving force behind the industrialisation process due to their important role played in economic development of western nations. The private entrepreneur is guided by the profit motive. He is responsible for the introduction of new commodities, new techniques of production, assembling the plant and equipment needed for the production, the labour force, managing and organising all the resources into a going concern. The private entrepreneur acts as an innovator who revolutionises the entire method of production. These are the activities that help the process of industrialisation and economic development. In the new liberalised scenario that has emerged after the announcement of the New Industrial Policy 1991, private sector has been assigned the dominant role in industrial development.

2. **Extensive Modern Industrial Sector:** A number of modern industries have been set up in the private sector. From the pre-independence period important consumer industries were set up in this sector. With the opportunities offered by the market forces industries like paper industry, sugar industry, cotton textile industry and edible oil industry has been set up in private sector. These industries were highly suitable for private sector as they ensured early returns and required less capital for establishment. After Independence, a number of consumer goods industries were set

up in the private sector and due to it today India is practically self-reliant in its requirements for consumer goods.   In case of intermediate goods and machines industries like chemical industries (paints, varnishes, plastics, etc.) and manufacturing machine tools (machinery and plants, ferrous and non-ferrous metals, rubber, paper etc.) have been set up in the private sector.

3. **Private Sector-the Dominant Sector:** Despite the rapid progress of the public sector in the period of planning, private sector is the dominant sector in the Indian economy.

   • Regarding the total number of companies- 89.6 percent companies were in the private sector and only 10.4 percent were in the public sector (as on March 31, 2009).

   • Regarding the manufacturing sector – 83.7 percent were in the private sector and only 16.3 percent were in the public sector (as on March 31, 2009).

   • Regarding employment – private sector's share is much higher in terms of employment, as out of 62.5 lakh persons engaged in manufacturing sector (31, March 2010) as many as 51.84 lakh persons were working in private sector.

4. **Potentialities in the Small Sector:** In India all small and cottage industries are in the private sector.   Small *and* cottage industries have an important role to play in the industrial field.   These industries employ labour-intensive techniques and hence provide employment opportunities.   In small scale industries personal initiative plays a decisive role.   With the help of small capital, the small entrepreneur uses his resources efficiently to earn maximum profit.   Such management is not available to public sector.   Government initiatives are supporting the private sector.   Industrial estates have been set up at various places where all facilities are provided under one roof to the small-scale industries.   They are provided loans at concessional rates of interest and marketing outlets.   Further, the government has reserved a large number of items for production in the small-scale sector.

Importance of Private Sector: Following are the merits/significance of private sector:

1. **Equilibrium Price:** The price is determined by the fair play of demand and supply of goods which are generally lower than the arbitrarily set monopoly prices. The businessmen and consumers prefer competitive prices, rather than controlled prices or monopoly prices.

2. **Rational Allocation of Resources:** The business is run with profit-motive. Hence, it results in rational and realistic approach towards obtaining and using the resources. That is, there is less wastage of scarce resources.

3. **Variety of Production:** There is scope for innovation, research and development because of free competition. It leads to the production of variety of products within the resources available.

4. **Consumer's Sovereignty:** The investment and production is directed to meet the demands of the consumers. Consumer's demand becomes the guidelines to the direction of production and prices to be fixed. Due to competition, consumer is treated as a king of the market.

5. **Efficiency:** The private sector is cost-conscious and profit-motivated. Hence, every factor of production is used to its optimum. There is appreciation in the quality of the product. In other words, there is economic use of resources and maximisation of production.

6. **Institution of Private Property:** Private sector holds the right to possess enjoy and dispose of private property. It helps economic development through capital formation.

7. **Spirit of Competition:** Private sector gets freedom of investment and production. Competition exists among the different firms in an industry.

8. **Decentralised Economy:** The private sector has freedom to take decisions on the economic activities within the broad framework of the rules of the government.

Limitations (Problems) of Private Sector:

The Private Sector suffers from certain drawbacks, as given below:

1. **Deficit in trade:** A large number of private sector companies have been resorting to massive imports in the post-liberalisation phase to upgrade their technology in a bid to brace up to global competition. Consequently, their import expenditures have increased at a much faster rate than their export earnings. This has pushed up the country's trade deficit.

2. **Declining share of net value added in total output:** Net value added is the amount generated over and above the cost of raw materials which go to the production system after making provisions for depreciation charges. Net value added in total output shows the industrial efficiency. Many industries in the private sector have reported a fall in the share of net value added in output. This decline means that the same amount of raw materials has generated less output and thus refers to its declining efficiency.

3. **Industrial disputes:** The private sector enterprises suffer from more industrial disputes, as compared to public sector enterprises. Differences and conflicts between the owners and employees regarding wages, bonus, retrenchment and other issues frequently emerge. There are Boards like Arbitration Boards, Works Committees, etc., for settlement of industrial disputes. Industrial disputes often result in strikes, lock-outs, gherao, etc., which results in loss of valuable man-days and productivity activity suffers.

4. **Profit-motive and Negligence towards Social Overheads:** In private sector industrialists operate with the sole motive of maximising profits due to which they are interested in investing only in those industrial sectors where quick profit generation is possible. They tend to invest in consumer goods industries and ignore investments that are crucial for building up a strong industrial infrastructure. It has been the public sector that has stepped in to invest in infrastructure and capital goods industries.   The responsibility of developing the capital goods and basic industries and industrial infrastructure, such as electricity and power, transportation, communications, etc., the private sector concentrated on consumer goods industries where investments were low and profits high. Thus, in the initial phase of industrial development the private sector was not willing to shoulder the responsibility of a prime mover of economic development process.

    Further, private sector having sole motive of profit-maximisation may lead to malpractices or non-competitive pricing policy by taking advantage of imperfections in the market. Through high sales propaganda the consumer is victimised.

5. **Inequalities of Income:** The competition of freedom of investment, production and the right to possess, use and dispose of property, results in concentration of economic power in a few hands and creates inequalities in the economy.

6. *Wastage of Competition:* To remain in the competitive business, the private sector players practice immoral and unethical measures that leads to wastage of resources and consumers have to pay the price for it.

7. **Cyclical Fluctuations:** A capitalist or private sector leads the economy in cyclical fluctuations due the uncertainties involved in its economic activities. During boom period private sector leads the investment more than full employment and during depression there is no optimistic attitude in their investment i.e. the private sector shy's away from investment.

8. **Exploitation of Workers:** With labour surplus in the economy, in India, workers are paid less than their marginal productivity. The workers cannot bargain for better working and living conditions due to competition and concentration of economic power. The workers are exploited through low wages, bad working conditions etc.

9. **Emphasis on consumer durables sector:** Even in the consumer goods sector, the focus of the private sector is on the elite consumer groups, such as consumer electronics and automobiles, due to the ample purchasing power with this group. Thus, the production pattern is skewed in favour of the relatively small richer sections of the society. Some economists are of the view that leads to wastage of the economic surplus on unnecessary industrial activities while the 'core' economic activities suffer. In other words, it leads to 'distortions in production structure'.

10. **Monopoly and concentration:** The monopoly organisations are strengthened and concentration of wealth and economic power in a few hands increases. These tendencies have become stronger by the substantial liberalisation of industrial policy which has enabled the large business houses to amass considerable wealth with the result that concentration of economic power has further increased.

11. **Industrial sickness:** This is a serious problem facing the small, medium and large enterprises in the private sector. Substantial amount of loanable funds of the financial institutions is locked up in sick industrial units causing not only wastage of resources but also affecting the healthy growth of the industrial economy adversely. Industrial sickness is caused by internal and external factors. Factors that are not under the control of the unit are power cuts, market fluctuations, government policies, etc. And factors under the control of the unit that are mismanaged and leads to industrial sickness are production, management, finance and so on.

12. **Threat from foreign competition:** The New Economic Policy of 1991 that unleashed the liberalisation process has opened up the gates to foreign investors and the government has progressively introduced the measures to 'open up' the economy to foreign competition. This process of globalisation and 'integration' of the Indian economy with the world economy has led to an unequal competition – a competition between 'giant multinationals' and 'dwarf Indian enterprises'. It soon came to be realised that opening up the Indian economy to foreign competition meant not only more and cheaper imports and more foreign investment but also opportunities to the MNCs to raid and takeover their enterprises. Even the large Indian enterprises are just pygmies compared to the multinational corporations. In short it is an issue of unequal competition between MNCs and Indian enterprises.

5.5 Public Sector Enterprises: Role, Functions and Problems

The state in India has always been undertaking certain economic activities like construction of roads and bridges, irrigational projects etc. But as yet no basic philosophy guided the state as to which economic activities the state should undertake and which it should not. The British rulers, who were looking after the administration of India, were trained in the economics of the English Classical School and thus, roughly up to 1914 minimum role was assigned for the state and there was adoption of the policy of 'laissez faire'.

However, the 'Great Depression' of 1929 and the publication of 'The General Theory' by **J. M. Keynes** in 1936 which pleaded for a positive role of the state in the economic activities. This influenced the Government of Great Britain and in turn the Government of India and its economic policy to a certain extent. Independence of the country in August 1947 put a radically different perspective so far as the public sector and its objectives and role are concerned.

It is essential that an underdeveloped nation which aims at achieving the goal of rapid economic development through economic planning and establishment of a socialist pattern of society should give a significant place to the public sector in its economy.

Objectives of the Public Sectors in India: The main objectives of the public sector in India are as follows:

1. To undertake economic activities those are strategically important for the growth of the economy.
2. To provide basic infrastructural facilities like roads and other means of communication, power, water, telegraph, telephone etc. which are so essential for the rapid economic development of the country.
3. To promote rapid economic development by investing in capital goods sector. Investment in capital goods sector is discouraging by private sector due to long gestation period in this sector.
4. To achieve balanced regional development by undertaking industrial development in backward areas and providing therein employment opportunities, raising standard of living etc.
5. To reduce inequalities of income and wealth.
6. To avoid concentration of economic power in a few private hands, this could take place if industries were owned and managed by private individuals.
7. To create increasing employment opportunities, raise per capita income of the people and ensure reasonable standard of living.
8. To establish and continue to have control over the vital sectors of the economy such as basic and heavy industries.

Role and Function of the Public Sector in India:

No single measure would be appropriate to estimate role of the public sector in the Indian economy. It is, thus, desirable to use a few indicators such as employment, investment, capital formation and capital stock, savings etc. Public sector has played a definite positive role in the economy.

1. **Public Sector in laying a Strong Base of Industrialisation:** By establishing industries like iron and steel metals, electricity, atomic energy, petroleum, heavy machinery, chemicals etc. the public sector in India has laid a strong base for the rapid industrialisation of the country. That is, the state took the responsibility for the development of key industries and rest of the industries were left to the private sector. In turn, the strong industrial foundation has helped in developing a number of capital goods and consumer goods industries in the country. Public sector has played an important role in developing and diversifying industrial production. It has helped the private sector to grow by providing infrastructure facilities, machinery and other capital equipments such as spares and energy.

In short, the credit for a strong base of industrialisation has to be given to the public sector. Even after the introduction of economic reforms, private sector has not increased as expected, thus the public sector has been suggested to take up the responsibility of infrastructure development.

2. **Removal of Regional Disparities:** The government in India has sought to use its power of setting up of industries as a means of removing regional disparities in industrial development. In the pre-Independence period, industrial progress of the country was restricted in and around the port towns of Mumbai, Kolkata and Chennai, while other parts of the country lagged far behind. Thus, a major proportion of public sector investment was directed towards backward states. All the four major steel plants in the public sector – Bhilai Steel Plant, Durgapur Steel Plant, Rourkela Steel Plant and Bokaro Steel Plant – were set up in the backward States. The objective was to unleash a propulsive mechanism in them and cause economic development of the neighbourhood. These considerations also guided the location of machinery and machine tools factories, aircraft, transport equipment, fertiliser plants, etc.

3. **Public Sector in Export Promotion:** Public sector undertakings have helped promote exports considerably and earn valuable foreign exchange needed to import defence equipment, advanced technology and also essential products like fertilizers, oilseeds, petroleum products etc.

Thus, some public sector units have done much to promote India's exports. In the field of export promotion public enterprises such as the State Trading Corporation, Hindustan Steel Limited, Hindustan Machine Tools etc. have done a commendable job. For instance, the metal ores have become the second largest single item on our list of exports. Further, considerable success has been achieved in increasing the exports of Indian handicrafts, light engineering goods and many new items of exports.

4. **Public Sector in Import Substitution:** By producing goods and services which earlier used to be imported by India, public sector enterprises have helped save valuable foreign exchange and have also utilised indigenous resources, Indian Labour and have increased the country's self-reliance in some of the vital industrial sectors.

Some of the public sector enterprises like Hindustan Antibiotics Ltd., Indian Drugs and Pharmaceuticals Ltd. succeeded in removing the monopolistic hold of foreign concerns in the manufacture of drugs and pharmaceuticals and have helped India to save foreign exchange. In the same way, the Oil and Natural Gas Commission (ONGC) and the Indian Oil Corporation Ltd. (IOCL) are some of the public sector undertakings which have reduced considerably India's dependence on imports and to that extent made the country self – reliant in vital sectors.

Complete self-sufficiency may not be possible as present, as import substitution have not been substantial in certain vital sectors like steel, fertilisers, edible oil, etc. The performance in the case on these industries in import substitution is disappointing, particularly when there are adequate raw materials, capital resources and technical know-how available.

5. **Role of Public Enterprises in the Growth of Ancillary Industries:** Public enterprises have boosted the development of a large number of ancillary industries and small-scale modern industries. This has been made possible when the public enterprises review their programmes of production and stop production of such needed items which can be produced in the ancillary units without allowing their installed capacities to remain idle or even negatively affecting their production schedules. In other words, during the review of production programmes certain items are off loaded to ancillary units and at the same time public sector utilises their own capacity more effectively. This encourages the growth of ancillary industries.

6. **Development of Infrastructure:** The primary condition of economic development in any underdeveloped country is that the infrastructure should develop at a rapid rate. For example, agricultural development cannot be witnessed without sufficient expansion of irrigation facilities, power and energy. Industrialisation can be sustained with adequate development of transportation and communication facilities, fuel and energy, basic and heavy industries. After Independence, the private sector neither showed any inclination to develop it nor had any resources to make this possible as it was comparatively weak both financially and technically and thus was incapable of setting up heavy industry. This situation made the State's participation in industrialisation essential as it was the government who could enforce a large-scale mobilisation of capital, training of technicians, etc. Thus, the public sector has enabled the economy to develop a strong infrastructure for the future economic growth.

7. **Check Overconcentration of Economic Power:** In a capitalist economy where the public sector is practically non-existent or is of small-size, economic power gets concentrated in a few hands and inequalities of income and wealth increase. The expansion of public sector will help in putting a brake on the tendency towards concentration of wealth and economic power in the private sector.

Public sector can help in reducing inequalities in the economy in following ways: (a) profits of the public sector can be used directly by the government on the welfare programmes of the poorer sections of the community; (b) public sector can divert production machinery towards the production of mass consumption goods; (c) public sector can give better wages to the lower staff when compared to private sector and implement programmes of labour welfare, slum clearance, construction of colonies and townships, etc.; (d) public sector can adopt a discriminatory policy by supplying materials to small industrialists at low prices and big industrialists at high prices.

8. **Public Sector and Capital Formation:** The role of public sector in collecting savings and investing them during the planning era has been very important. During the First and Second Plans, of the total investment, 54 percent was in the public sector and the remaining in the private sector. With increasing trends of liberalisation, the share of public sector in total investment fell drastically to 34.3 percent in the 8th Plan and to further 29.5 percent in the 9th Plan. This reflects the increasing importance that is now being accorded to the private sector. The nationalised banks, State Bank of India, IDBI, Industrial Finance Corporation of India (IFCI), State Financial Corporations, LIC, UTI, etc., have played an important role in collecting savings and mobilisation of resources.

9. **Public Sector in Critical Areas:** Public sector has entered into a wide spectrum of industries and products. Most of these industries have a strategic importance in the Indian economy due to their high linkages. For example, its operations extend from basic and capital goods like steel, coal, heavy machinery, drugs and chemical fertilizers, consumer goods like textiles, hotel services etc. Most of these industries have a strategic importance in the Indian economy since they have high linkages. In highly critical areas such as copper, coal, petroleum products, hydro and steam turbines the share of public sector is 100 percent.

   In quite a large number of products the share of public sector ranges between 50 to 95 per cent.

10. **Contribution of Public Sector to the Exchequer:** Public sector enterprises have not only helped in generating internal resources but have made substantial contribution to Government exchequer through payment of corporate taxes, excise duty, customs duty and other duties. In other words, public enterprises help in mobilising funds for financing the needs for the planned development of the nation. Public enterprises contributed ₹ 27,570 crores during the 6th Plan that increased to ₹ 1,11,149 crores for the period 2002-03 to 2006-07, i.e., Tenth Plan. In 2010-11, Public sector contributed ₹ 1,56,124 crores to exchequer.

11. **Public Sector in Raising Internal Resources:** Internal resources comprise of depreciation and retained profits. Public sector has played an important role in generation of internal resources as they not only finance their own planned expansion and development, but also generate surplus for financing the needs of other priority sectors in the country.

It is observed that during the Sixth Plan (1980-85), internal resources amounted to ₹ 14,710 crores were generated. During the year 2001-02, internal resources generated was ₹ 52,545 crores. During the Tenth Plan (2002-03 to 2006-7) total internal resources generated were of order of ₹ 3, 95, 686 crores. It is indeed, a very encouraging situation wherein the Central public sector has succeeded in generating internal resources.

12. **Public Sector in Employment:** Public sector employment includes:
   (a) Government administration and defence and other Government services like health, education, activities that promote economic development;
   (b) Public sector units owned by Centre, State and Local government. Employment in the public sector is confined to the organised sector; public sector employs 62.4 percent of the workers employed in organised sector of the Indian economy. The share of public sector in total employment in the organised sector- public plus private – shows that in transport and communications, electricity, gas and water and construction, the share of public sector is in the range of 95 to 98 percent, a situation of total dominance. In manufacturing the share of the public sector was about 27 percent. In an overall sense, the public sector is a big employer, 62.4 percent, in so far as the organised sector of the Indian economy is concerned.

Hence, from every aspect, the public sector has grown in importance and has come to occupy a prominent place in the Indian economy.

Problems of Public Sector:

It would be unreasonable to argue that all is well in the public enterprises. As, even after substantial achievements of the public sector undertakings in India, it would be better to examine critically some of the important problems of public sector units. This would help to devise and adopt measures for improving their efficiency and enable them to fulfil their various socio-economic objectives.

The main points which need consideration are:

1. **Under-utilisation of the installed Capacity:** It has been found that the optimum capacity of the industries is not utilised. For example, during 2005-06 out of 203 units, 103 units (51 per cent) of all manufacturing units had recorded capacity utilisation of more than 75 percent. On the other hand, 33 public undertakings recorded capacity utilisation between 50 to 75 per cent and 67 operated below 50 per cent utilisation of their installed capacity. This is certainly not an optimum situation. Hence, this calls for remedial measures after knowing the causes of under-utilisation of installed capacity.

2. **Over-capitalisation:** Public sector units suffer from over-capitalisation. As financial resources are easily available from the government, many public sector projects are charged with over-capitalisation, showing capital-output ratio unduly unfavourable. This locks up the precious investment funds in a capital starved country like India. It leads to waste of valuable resources from the community's point of view and depriving some of the much-needed funds.

   In connection with the charges of over-capitalisation the Study Team mentioned, "the causes leading to over-capitalisation can be traced to inadequate planning, delays and avoidable expenditure during construction, surplus machine capacity, tied aid resulting in the compulsion to purchase imported equipment on a non-competitive basis, expensive turn-key contracts, bad location of projects and the provision of housing and other amenities on liberal scale".

3. **Interference by Political Factors in Location of the Unit:** In many cases, it has been observed that political factors influence decisions about location of projects. **Besant C. Raj** has shown that government's investment decisions relating to public sector enterprises are often not preceded by a detailed evaluation of the nature of potential demand, import content, availability of technical and executive personnel and economic cost-benefit analysis. As a result that many a time's faulty decisions in this regard are taken often under political pressure. A classical example of this political but irrational approach is the decision of the Central Government. It was MIG aircraft project. It was put into two parts and they were to be located in two separate States - Nasik and Koraput. These two locations are over 900 kms. apart. Such a faulty decision on location was to satisfy two powerful political bosses from two states.

4. **Inefficiency in Management:** To improve the overall performance of public sector enterprises, one of the crucial factors is managerial efficiency. Many public enterprises are characterised by inefficient management. This is because of non-availability of top executive personnel.

   For efficiency in industrial enterprises it is essential that:

   (a) Operational decisions are prompt. This requires a lot of autonomy and flexibility of operations in the public enterprises.

   (b) Secondly, it is necessary that there is delegation of authority, from the top management to the lower levels for operational efficiency. However, in public units there has been general failure to define responsibilities.

   (c) Thirdly, experienced persons at the top positions are essential for successful operation of public enterprises. And, public enterprises are sarcastically referred to as 'colonies for bureaucrats'.

   (d) An unfortunate practice has been to use bureaucrats as Chairman, Managing Directors and managers of public sector units.

It is found that many of them are not really qualified to run industrial enterprises. For efficiency in public sector enterprises, the Government should progressively shift professionalised management in these enterprises.

5. **Increase in Costs of Construction Due to Delay in Completion of Projects:** Many study reports point out that many of the projects undertaken by public sector units take longer time to complete than was initially planned. Due to delays in completion, the cost of the project was also revised upwards. Most of the delay in construction and hence increase in costs has been due to poor and inadequate project planning. An example of delay in construction and rise in construction costs is of Trombay Fertilizer Project. It took 6 to 7 years to complete the project as against the estimated time-schedule of 3 years.

   Thus, it is necessary to prepare comprehensive construction plans to avoid delays, rise in costs and also to avoid additional burden on the scarce resources.

6. **Inappropriate Price Policy:** The sole objective of profit-maximisation is not the guiding principle of public sector enterprises. They have to keep in mind the social implications of its price policy. Because, it would be suicidal for the overall growth of the economy to fix high prices of steel, oil, fertilizers. With such a socialist objective, public sector units are pressurised to keep the prices low even when costs and prices have been rising. This affects commercial profitability. In short, pricing policies are irrational in public sector units.

   However, it is being realised that profit should be recognised as an index of efficiency. There are some public sector units which operate to protect consumer's interests and here profit should be least important. Yet there are another group of public units which are basic to others and assist in all round development of the economy. Here too the prices are fixed without consideration to high profits. The third group of public sector units is that where high profit policy can safely be adopted. By classifying the public enterprises with their objectives, pricing policies can be more rational.

7. **Unduly Heavy Overhead Expenditure:** Often unduly heavy expenditure was incurred on social overheads such as establishing of townships, quarters for workers etc. While these were necessary, the question is whether the expenditure on such items could have been avoided, minimised and whether the country could at a particular stage of its economic development afford such social overhead expenditure.

8. **Excess use of Man-Power Resources:** There is poor man-power planning and this is clearly seen in the inadequate arrangements for training and education of workers. Various reasons have led to the exit of personnel from public sector to the private

sector units – unsatisfactory salary, absence of incentives to staff etc. It has been suggested that professional and technical persons of the unit should be trained and induced into management. It is also essential that Government should take steps to improve industrial relations as indiscipline among the workers and poor management-labour relations have adversely affected public sector enterprises.

9. **Lack of Co-ordination among Different Public Sector Enterprises:** It is necessary that there is co-ordination among various public enterprises to attain greater efficiency and for maximising returns from them. As the output of one unit is the input of some other units, better co-ordination is essential for smooth functioning. For example, the performance of steel plants and power houses in the public sector depends upon coal production and transportation of coal to different production centres of steel and electricity. Failure in any one of the units will have an unfavourable effect on the production of all the other related units. Proper and effective co-ordination among various public sector undertakings would help reduce excessive stock of inventory and shortage of vital inputs. Co-ordination of activities can also be worked out in areas such as material management, personnel, inventory control, finance, research and development etc.

10. **Research and Development:** It is noted that R and D has received scanty attention in public sector units. R and D will help the industrial units increase their efficiency, improve quality, bring reduction in the cost of production. Public sector units play safe by sticking to conventional and traditional methods of production. Such a conservative attitude would not be helpful in the long run.

To conclude, it is true that all the public sector units are not functioning efficiently. However, the competitiveness of the private and public sector projects should act as the motivating mechanism and help improving efficiency in both the sectors.

5.6 Disinvestment Policies

In simple language disinvestment can be understood as follows – "Investment refers to the conversion of money or cash into securities, debentures, bonds or any other claims on money. And disinvestment involves the conversion of money claims or securities into money or cash".

Disinvestment can be defined as the action of an organisation or government selling or liquidating an asset or subsidiary.

In general disinvestment typically refers to sale from the government, partly or fully, of a government-owned enterprise. A company or a government will typically disinvest an asset either as a strategic move for the company or for raising resources to meet general or specific needs.

Disinvestment is the process through which privatisation could take place. Since the beginning of 1980s quite a large number of public enterprises incurred losses year after year. It was argued that the State should not be called upon to meet the losses of these enterprises out of tax payer's money. As a result, the question of privatisation of the public sector was debated.

Objectives/rationale for Disinvestment:

The New Economic Policy initiated in July 1991 clearly indicated that Public Sector Undertakings (PSUs) had shown a negative rate of return on capital employed. Inefficient PSUs had become a drag on the Government's resources turning to be more of liabilities to the Government than being assets. Many undertakings traditionally established as pillars of growth had become a burden on the economy. The national gross domestic product and gross national savings were also getting adversely affected by low returns from PSUs.

- The need for the Government to get rid of these units and to concentrate on core activities was identified.
- The government was of the view that it should move out of non-core businesses, especially the ones where the private sector had now entered in a significant way.
- Disinvestment was also seen by the government to raise funds for meeting general or specific needs.

In this direction, the Government adopted the 'Disinvestment Policy'. The Ministry of Disinvestment outlines the following as the main objectives:

(i)   To reduce public debt;

(ii) Stemming further outflow of scarce public resources for sustaining the unviable non-strategic PSUs;

(iii) To improve public finances;

(iv) To encourage wider share of ownership. Transferring the commercial risk to the private sector wherever the private sector is willing and able to step in;

(v)   To depoliticise non-essential services;

(vi) Releasing other tangible and intangible resources, such as, large manpower currently locked up in managing public sector enterprises, and their time and energy, for deployment in high priority social sectors that are short of such resources;

(vii) To introduce competition and market discipline.

Importance of Disinvestment

The importance of disinvestment lies in utilisation of funds for:

- For investing in the economy to encourage spending;
- Financing the increasing fiscal deficit;
- Financing large-scale infrastructure development;
- For social programmes like health and education;
- For retiring Government debt, almost 40 to 45 percent of the Centre's revenue receipts go towards repaying public debt/interest.

Disinvestment also assumes significance due to the prevalence of an increasingly competitive environment, which makes it difficult for many PSUs to operate profitably. It has led to rapid erosion of value of the public assets making it critical to disinvest early to realise a high value.

Critique of Disinvestment (Arguments For and Against Disinvestment): Disinvestment of Strategic and Non-Strategic

The supporters of disinvestments argue that it is not the business of the Government to be in business. They believe that for strategic sectors like arms and ammunitions, defence equipment, atomic energy and railway transport, the Government should run the PSEs. For non-strategic areas the government should not run any public sector enterprises. In USA, too, the oil sector is considered strategic. Hence, it would be advisable to reconsider the areas which deserve to be included in the strategic sector. Industries vitally important for the economy need continuance in the public sector. Another strategic area to be under PSEs is power generation. It is PSU – Bharat Heavy Electricals Limited (BHEL) – that has beaten world leaders like Siemens, GEC. The disappointing experience with ENRON, an MNC contracted to enhance power generation, should not lead us to conclude that BHEL is a non-strategic.

Issue of Profit-Making Public Enterprises

Another issue of debate is privatisation of profit-making public enterprises. It would be of importance to understand the rationale of disinvestment and wisdom of disinvestment of highly profitable public sector enterprises like Videsh Sanchar Nigam Limited (VSNL). Another firm disinvested was the IBP.

Was the disinvestment undertaken for these two firms due to avoidance of loss and were these firms loss-making organisations? Had it been a case of an inefficient concern, the Tatas would not have given a bid for a price per share at 20 percent premium over the share market price. Disinvestment in this direction is taking the government in direction of creating 'private monopoly'. It can thus be said that the entire policy of privatisation of VSNL, a highly profit-making public sector giant, was irrational.

The other public sector, IBP, has been taken over by the IOC (33.6 percent stake) for the highest bid of ₹ 1,154 crores. It has been argued that this is not privatisation but in its name it is a means to achieve certain ends. All this is based on the belief that the efficiency of the private sector is taken for granted. S. R. Mohnot while comparing public and private sectors mention that nearly 62 percent public sector companies had declared dividends exceeding 10 percent, in the case of the private sector companies, only 35 percent had declared dividends exceeding 10 percent.

It proves that in the post-liberalisation period, the performance of Central Public Sector Enterprises (CPSEs) has been progressively improving. Net profit after taxes of the CPSEs was

5.4 per cent in 1997-98 and has risen to 12.3 percent in 2006/07. This performance is commendable as compared to the private sector which did not do better. It all implies that the public sector of the post-reform period is no longer the public sector of the 70s and 80s.

- PSEs like Indian Oil Corporation have become global giants with excellent record of performance.
- The Disinvestment Department had another issue was about privatisation of public sector oil giants HPCL and BPCL. It was of the view that co-operatives like IFCO and KRIBHCO should not be allowed to bid for these oil giants.
- Public sector giants like Gas Authority of India Limited (GAIL) and Indian Oil Corporation (IOC) should not be allowed to participate in the bid.
- The Disinvestment Ministry's intentions to permit private sector – Indian or Foreign – alone to participate in the sale of HPCL and BPCL. The argument was that the sale of PSU to another government –owned enterprise goes against the grain of privatisation, which implies change of ownership.
- This view was challenged by many Ministers even within the NDA government. They believe that competition should be allowed between the public, private and co-operative sectors.
- Why should government privatise PSUs with good track-record? To push sale to raise revenue shows no logic in disinvestment of such PSUs.
- Some of the PSUs have been designated as Navratnas or mini-navratnas, then why privatise?
- NALCO (National Aliminium Co. Ltd.) has been taken for disinvestment when it shows a profit of ₹ 656 crores in 2000-01. BPCL (₹ 820 crores), HPCL (₹ 1,088 crores), Shipping Corporation of India (₹ 383 crores), Engineers India Ltd. (₹ 124 crores).

Issue of Loss-Making Public Enterprises
- There is no opposition to the privatisation of loss-making units. The Government should shed their load and rid itself of the burden of these enterprises.
- If logic followed is that mere change of ownership can bring about great change in the culture of an organisation, then the private sector should take over the loss making concerns and convert them into profit-making organisations.

Thus, the Disinvestment Ministry should be cautious of transferring PSUs which are milch cows, to the private sector. A write-up by Mr. Jyotiraditya Scindia, in Hindustan Times, 8 October 2002 – *"We should provide flexibility to companies to raise funds and grow, rather than sell them off so cheaply. The government can't throttle companies with the dilution argument and then blame them for inefficiency".*

Method for Disinvestment

The Government did not seem to have a clear policy on the methodology of disinvestment.

- Open Auction Sale: The government followed the policy of open auction sale and allowed NRIs and other persons legally permitted to hold equity to participate. This resulted in realisation of ₹ 4,843 crores as against the target of ₹ 4,000 crores in 1994-95.

- Strategic Partner: In 1999-2000 the government shifted the policy to strategic sale. It was argued that the public offer method is slow and would take very long to complete the process of disinvestment of all PSUs. However, the critics were of the opinion that public offering could succeed in the U.K., France, Malaysia, China, South Africa, Spain and Germany, what prevents its adoption in India.

- In case of HPCL and BPCL – two different approaches were adopted by the government. In case of BPCL it adopted the public offering methodology and in case of HPCL it was strategic investor.

- It was also argued that Government when it follows public offering of shares, it can unload a part of the equity and still continue its hold over the PSU, but by strategic partner it transfer the management of a company to a private investor even when he owns a minority stake in the company.

- Naturally the public offering method has logical superiority and the Government should shed its policy of strategic partner, once and for all, to save itself from public criticism.

Creation of Private Monopoly:

- By accepting Tatas as strategic partners in VSNL and Reliance in IPCL, the Government substituted State Monopolies with Private Monopolies. As known Monopoly – whether public or private – is undesirable. However, public sector is relatively less harmful than a private sector monopoly. Public sector monopoly is accountable to the Parliament, but a private sector monopoly is not accountable and can exploit the consumer to a great extent.

Valuation of PSUs for Disinvestment:

- Since the process has started, the problem of valuation of PSUs slated for disinvestment has been engaging the attention of Government and the Public Accounts Committee (PAC).

- The PAC held the then Union Finance Minister Dr. Manmohan Singh, and the then Industry Secretary, Mr. Suresh Kumar, responsible for under-realisation of the value of the shares divested in 1991-92 and quantified the loss to the order of ₹ 3,000 crores in 1991-92, even the government has raised till March 1993, ₹ 4,950 crores by disinvestment.

- It is true that efforts have been made to streamline procedures for valuation of PSUs but the vested interests within the Government have been manipulating valuation process to the benefit of private companies by privatising a number of profit-making PSUs at price well below the intrinsic worth of assets. Mr. Paranjoy Guha Thakurta, a well known journalist in his article gave some examples in this regard:

  (a) The Comptroller and Auditor General (CAG) of India in his report has estimated that the value of assets of recently privatised BALCO was underestimated to the extent of ₹ 300 crores.

  (b) The Birla-group-controlled Zuari Marco Phosphates Private Ltd., after having paid ₹ 151.7 crores to the government for purchasing 74 percent shares of Paradeep Phosphates Ltd., wanted almost the entire amount back on the ground that the government wrongly calculated the financial position of the former PSU in Orissa.

  (c) In January 2001, the Hindustan Lever Ltd. (HIL) claimed ₹ 12.6 crores from the government on account of excess payment, after having paid ₹ 105 crores for acquiring majority stake in Modern Food Industries. After detaining this amount, HIL has put forth another claim of ₹ 4.8 crores from the government.

  (d) In June 2001, the government received ₹ 83 crores from Batra Hospitality for the sale of Centaur Hotel neat Mumbai airport. In four months time this hotel was sold to Sahara India Group for ₹ 115 crores (a hike of 38.6 percent). Here the government needs to answer as to why was the hotel under-valued and was there no lock period? It only raises the doubt about the role of bureaucracy which cleverly puts Government money into the private pocket of the so-called strategic partner.

Besides the above few examples there may be many more with the Disinvestment Ministry. These examples also raise several issues about the valuation of assets of PSU slated for disinvestment.

Discrepancy in valuation: Why there is sharp discrepancies in valuation?

- In case of Vadodara unit of the former PSU, IPCL (Indian Petrochemicals Corporation Ltd.), when there was talk about IOC going in for the bid of this corporation KMPG valued it for ₹ 1,234 crores while Deloittes Harkins valued it at ₹ 3,456 crores (180 percent higher than KMPG). The Government permitted Reliance Petro-investment to acquire control over the company by paying ₹ 1,491 crores and thus the Ambanies were able to control 70 to 90 percent of the Indian Market for a wide variety of petrochemicals products. The doubt arises as to why a firm valued for ₹ 3,456 crores was sold out for merely ₹ 1,491 crores.

- The most striking drawback of the methodology of valuation of assets of PSUs is that lands belonging to the PSUs have been left completely out of the exercise of valuation on the false and patently unjustified statement that the large tracts of land owned by PSUs do not earn any 'income' and hence they need not be valued.
- The government has taken the position that land value is computed in most of the cases when the PSU concerned is disinvested or sold to another party. This is downright dishonesty. 127 acres of land attached with VSNL in south Delhi has no intrinsic value since it does not, as stated by the merchant banking valuers, yield any 'income'. It would be wrong to ignore nearly a similar plot by VSNL in Chattarpur, besides 700 acres in Pune. If market value of the land in these areas is taken as the basis of valuation of land, then the total assets value of the PSU would show an improvement.
- Mr. Thakuta concludes: "Until issues of valuation are sorted out, the government cannot expect political consensus on its controversial privatisation programme".

Utilisation of the Proceeds:

- So far the Government has been putting the proceeds of disinvestment into a black hole known as the Consolidated Fund of India from which it met the budget deficit.
- The criticism of the disinvestment policy follows that the funds raised by selling family silver were used to pay the butler. As such, it was a case of meeting budget deficit by selling PSUs.
- The advice of the late Dr. Mahbu-ul-Haq, UNDP expert was: "Do not use sale proceeds to finance budget deficits – retire national debt". However, the Government has been ignoring this advice.

Concern over Disinvestment:

- Former Defence Minister George Fernandes felt so strongly against the reckless pursuit of disinvestment that he even wrote a letter to the Prime Minister on August 27, 2002. The excerpts from his letter:
- *"I believe that the objective for disinvestment should be to benefit the public, the consumer and the investor, and at the same time, to improve competiveness and eliminate monopoly..."*
- *"Our Disinvestment Policy should, therefore, be to offer these companies to the public of India. The current system of strategic sales is tantamount to handing over the entities created with the wealth of the people of India to further enrich the already rich".*
- *"I understand that virtually the entire privatisation in the UK was to the public at large, i.e. the Airlines, the Steel Industry, the telecom Industry, the automobile Industry, the Gas and Petroleum Sector etc., were privatised by offering through the stock markets.*

- *Likewise I believe the privatisation of the same sectors in France including the Banking and Oil sectors were disinvested to the French public and not through strategic sales. Malaysia, China, South Africa, Spain and Germany also followed suit".*
- *In the transfer of VSNL and IPCL, we began created monopolies with Tata and Reliance. If we pursue the strategic sale route in the aluminium and petroleum sectors, it is very likely that we will create monopolies within these vital sectors of the economy. State monopolies will become private monopolies. Is this good for the Indian consumer?"*
- *"Another issue of concern is that even if strategic sales are allowed, the PSUs will not be allowed to bid. Strengthening the PSUs through strategic amalgamations/ purchases of each other prior to sales to the public could be a worthwhile route to consider".*

Besides the Former Defence Minister's comments, Swadeshi Jagran Manch had also been critical of the disinvestment policy of the NDA government:

- The issues were: is the Government classification of 1999 into strategic and non-strategic sectors correct?
- Is it desirable to disinvest profit-making public enterprises, while keeping the loss-making PSUs under state ownership?
- What should be the procedure for disinvestment – public offering through stock exchange or strategic sale to a private party?
- Should disinvestment create private monopoly in place of public monopoly?
- What should be the method of valuation of a PSU before a bid for disinvestment is made?
- Should PSUs be allowed to participate in the bids for disinvestment of PSUs?
- How should the proceeds from disinvestment be utilised?
- How should the interests of workers and employees be safeguarded?

To conclude, while the Congress initiated the process of economic reform with stress on privatisation, the BJP-led NDA Government, blatantly carried forward the banner of privatisation. In the process, the country had to pay enormous costs to meet the budget deficits by fleecing the healthy PSUs, the navratnas are also not spared.

Disinvestment : Scenario of Indian Mindset

- The Indian approach to disinvestments seems to have gone wrong being positioned in the middle between the doctrinarian extreme on the one end and the laissez-faire extreme on the other.
- The country seems to have lost both the opportunity and the direction.
- The pace is poor, lethargic, and lack lustre.
- While all political parties and economists believe in the principle of disinvestments/privatisation, they devise escape routes for non-implementation of it by taking recourse to statements such as "we agree in principle but differ in the details." Or "First bring in a strategic partner and then disinvest", or "it is videshi, swadeshi", or "First increase the equity base through a public offer and then disinvest".

- The industry and business express their doubts about raising such huge funds to buy out and acquire PSUs.
- The foreign investors are critical of the entire process and are often seen withdrawing from the bidding process.
- Thus, there is something seriously wrong in India's approach to disinvestment and implementation of the policy.

To conclude, the public sector enterprises' contribution to national development is widely acknowledged. Their poor financial return has been a matter of deep and enduring concern, particularly during the mid-1980s when for the first time the central government's current revenues were found inadequate to meet its current expenditure.

5.7 Micro, Small and Medium Enterprises (MSMEs): Role and Problems

In accordance with the provision of Micro, Small and Medium Enterprises Development (MSMED) Act, 2006 the Micro, Small and Medium Enterprises (MSMEs) are classified in two classes:

(a) **Manufacturing Enterprises:** The enterprises engaged in the manufacture or production of goods pertaining to any industry specified in the first schedule to the industries (Development and Regulation Act, 1951) or employing plant and machinery in the process of value addition to the final product having a distinct name or character or use. The manufacturing enterprises are defined in terms of investment in plant and machinery.

(b) **Service Enterprises:** The enterprises engaged in providing or rendering of services and are defined in terms of investment in equipment.

The limit for investment in plant and machinery/equipment for manufacturing/service enterprises are as under:

Manufacturing Sector	
Enterprises	**Investment in Plant and Machinery**
• Micro Enterprises	Does not exceed 25 lakh rupees.
• Small Enterprises	More than 25 lakh rupees but does not exceed 5 crore rupees.
• Medium Enterprises	More than 5 crore rupees but does not exceed 10 crore rupees.
Service Sector	
Enterprises	**Investment in Equipments**
• Micro Enterprises	Does not exceed 10 lakh rupees.
• Small Enterprises	More than 10 lakh rupees but does not exceed 2 crore rupees.
• Medium Enterprises	More than two crore rupees but does not exceed 5 crore rupees.

Small and Medium Enterprises (SMEs) in India

Before independence, India had only the rudiments of an industrial structure dominated by the consumer goods industries. Since the introduction of Five Year Plans, the industrial sector expanded rapidly. Since the initiation of planned development the economy has attained considerable diversification. The broad aims of the Plans have been to turn India into an industrial power. The strategy adopted involved the establishment of a heavy industrial base and consumer goods industry to self-sufficiency. As a result the industrial structure has been widely diversified covering broadly the entire range of consumer, intermediate and capital goods. A notable result has been the emergence of a new progressing middle class of technicians, managers and entrepreneurs.

Thus, with the advent of planned economy from 1951 and the subsequent industrial policy followed by Government of India, both planners and Government earmarked a **special role for small-scale industries and medium scale industries** in the Indian economy.

From 1951 to 1991, Government followed protective policy and hence gave due protection to both the sectors and particularly to small-scale industries. Till the nation adopted a policy of liberalisation, globalisation and privatisation (LPG), certain products were reserved for small-scale units. However, this list of products is decreasing with the change in economic climate and industrial policies.

SMEs always represented the model of socio-economic policies of Government of India. In other words, in the Indian economy scenario Government stressed on :

(a) Judicious use of foreign exchange for import of capital goods and inputs;

(b) Labour-intensive mode of production in labour surplus economy;

(c) Generation of employment;

(d) Non-concentration (i.e. diffusion) of economic power in the hands of few big houses;

(e) MRTP Act discouraging monopolistic practices of production and marketing;

(f) Effective contribution to foreign exchange earning of the nation with import-substitution operations;

(g) Encourage dispersion or avoid concentration of industrial activities in few geographical centres.

In view to the above said socio-economic policies of Government of India, it has been observed that by and large, SMEs in India met the expectations of the Government. In fact, SMEs developed in such a manner that it made possible for them to achieve the following objectives :

(a) SMEs **contributed** effectively and highly to **domestic production**.

(b) They require **low investments**.

(c) They contribute significantly to **export earnings**.

(d) SMEs have **operational flexibility**.

(e) They have an attribute of greater **location wise mobility**.

(f) In terms of raw material, intermediate goods etc. SMEs are **low intensive imports** i.e. they cause less burden on Government for imports.

(g) SMEs have capacities to develop appropriate **indigenous technology**. Such a technology is more adaptable to the Indian economy.

(h) SMEs produce goods which were imported earlier i.e. they assist in **import substitution**.

(i) SMEs contribute towards **defence production**.

(j) SMEs are **technology-oriented** industries.

(k) SMEs have **brought forth competitiveness** in domestic and export markets.

Limitations : However, SMEs suffer from following limitations :

1. In spite of credit expansion by various institutions, SMEs depend more on their own funds and borrowed funds from non-banking and non-government sector. Thus, SMEs generally have a **low capital base** to begin with.

2. SMEs are generally family business and leads to **concentration of functions** in one or two persons of the family or relatives or friends.

3. **Inadequate exposure to international environment** due to their limited activities mainly concentrated in domestic regions.

4. SMEs are **unable to face the impact of WTO regime**. In other words, the rules and regulations laid down by WTO with regard to international trade are difficult to cope with by SMEs.

5. SMEs with their limited capital base and conservative attitude have suffered due to **inadequate contribution towards Research and Development (R&D).**

6. There seems to be **lack of professionalism** in SMEs.

In spite of these short-comings, the SMEs have made remarkable contribution towards exports and technological development.

SMEs are growing at a significant pace. In fact, SMEs have been set up in almost all major sectors in the Indian industry. Some of the major sectors in which SMEs are contributing significantly are as follows :

- Food Processing,
- Engineering, Electricals, Electronics,
- Agricultural Inputs,
- Sports goods,
- Bio-engineering,
- Plastic Products,
- Computer Software,
- Leather and Leather products,

- Textiles and Garments,
- Chemicals and Pharmaceuticals,
- Electro-Medical equipments,
- Meat Products etc.

Due to liberalisation, privatisation and globalisation (LPG) together with WTO regime, Indian SMEs have been passing through a transitional period. SMEs are facing a tough time with slowing down of economy in India and abroad, particularly in USA and European Union, increased competition from China and also from a few low cost centres of production from foreign land.

Thus, it can be said that for these SMEs to withstand the present challenges and make valuable contribution to the Indian economy, the SMEs have to build up a strong technological base, have an international business outlook, competitive spirit and should be ready to restructure them.

SMEs in Maharashtra State

Maharashtra state has been always in the fore front of industrialisation and has followed progressive industrial policies and industry-friendly measures. SMEs are well guided and assisted through a network of District Industries Centre-DICs. Many SMEs promoted by local entrepreneurs as also by NRIs and foreigners have come up in Maharashtra covering a broad spectrum of industrial activity.

The quality of products of SMEs from Maharashtra is high as some of them have acquired technology from abroad, adequate budget is allotted for Research and Development operations and many units are promoted by techno-entrepreneurs.

In major sectors, such as Engineering, Electricals, Food Processing, Chemicals and Pharmaceuticals, a survey was undertaken of SMEs in certain important cities/regions.

1. **Western Maharashtra :** Pune, Kolhapur, Nasik, Ahmednagar.
2. **Konkan Region :** Ratnagiri, Sawantwadi.
3. **Marathwada :** Aurangabad, Latur, Beed, Nanded.
4. **Vidharbha :** Nagpur, Amravati.
5. **Greater Mumbai :** Thane, Mumbai, Belapur.

About 23 SME units were surveyed on the following points :

(a) Set up of the unit.
(b) Management.
(c) Technical set up.
(d) Product profile.
(e) Turnover and exports.
(f) Scientific manpower.

Observation of Selected SMEs in Maharashtra :

1. **Electrical Industry :** Maharashtra state enjoys a competitive advantage in electrical sector e.g. switch-gears, electrical motors, transformers, electrical home appliances, pollution control equipment, lighting fixtures and lamps etc. This industry will continue to remain large and crucial industry segment, in Maharashtra, to support industry and household. Maharashtra and Gujarat will continue to dominate this industry as more than half of the nation's output and value addition is from here.

   The Government of Maharashtra has taken effective steps by introducing stringent pollution control laws.

2. **Food Processing Industry :** This is an important sector of the Indian economy. The food industry contributes about 18% of India's manufacturing output and around 5% of total industrial investment. The important segments in this industry comprising of packaged and branded food products are witnessing rapid growth accompanied by intense competition. Nearly, 52% of the Indian household budget is spent on food items and the share of processed food entering the market is expected to rise rapidly.

   Maharashtra has 10 to 15% production share of agro produce related to processed industry. Major units in Maharashtra include :

   (a) Fruit and vegetables;

   (b) Bakery products;

   (c) Dairy products;

   (d) Fish products;

   (e) Cereals.

3. **Pharmaceuticals Industry :** Indian pharmaceutical industry has been nurtured to a large extent by Indian patent laws, which recognised only process patents. Though India could build a strong base and infrastructure for production of medicines but it never cared to spend on Research and Development. It is an expenditure of less than 3 per cent of the India's turnover.

   In terms of exports of drugs and pharmaceuticals, it has increased from ₹ 2256.6 crores in 1994-95 to ₹ 3177.7 crores in 1995-96 to remarkable ₹ 4090.3 crores in 1996-97 showing an annual growth rate of 34.4 per cent.

   Many companies have also been upgrading their facilities to match internationally recognised standards of ISO 9002 certifications.

   Maharashtra is a major centre for both production and exports of basic drugs and pharmaceuticals in the country. The state's share in all India production of drugs is about 40 per cent and in all India exports it is about 33 per cent.

4. **Chemical Industry :** Maharashtra enjoys a competitive advantage in certain chemical industries such as Agro chemicals, Fertilizers, Pesticides, Dyes etc. In state of Maharashtra chemical industry will continue to remain a large and a crucial industry catering to the needs of agriculture, household consumption, defence requirements, industrial uses etc.

5. **Engineering Industry in Maharashtra :** Engineering industry in the state is highly diversified and produces a large range of parts to industrial machinery to industrial castings and forging.

    The industry which was earlier concentrated in the Mumbai-Pune belt has spread all over the states - Nagpur, Aurangabad, Nasik and Kolhapur.

    The products which have high potential of exports from Maharashtra include two/three wheelers automobile parts, machine tools, industrial machinery, steel tubes, seamless tubes, switch gears etc. It accounts for over 21 per cent of total exports of engineering products in the year 1996-97.

    The major competing nations for most of the engineering goods exported from the state are Japan, China, Taiwan, South Korea etc.

To conclude, while surveying some units of SMEs it was found that there was a proper coverage of all regions of Maharashtra except Vidarbha region which has two industrial regions- Nagpur and Amravati.

Further, small-scale units are defined as those producing units whose investments in plant and machinery is up to ₹ 10 million. But, there is no clear cut definition of medium scale units and these are always considered as between small and large-scale units.

SMEs were found to be organised, professionally managed and were aware of their techno-commercial strength and their core competence. These units have been quite successful in domestic market but only few have been exposed to overseas markets.

INTRODUCTION

The abbreviation SME occurs commonly in the European Union and in international organisation, such as the World Bank, the United Nations and the WTO. The term Small and Medium-sized Businesses (SMBs) is predominantly used in the USA. In the European Union and USA, SMBs are companies whose head count or turnover falls below certain limits. The business is classified as per the number of employees employed in the business. In South Africa the term SMME – Small, Medium and Micro Enterprises is used. Elsewhere in Africa, they use MSME – Micro, Small and Medium Enterprises.

In India, the sector is generally referred to as the Micro, Small and Medium Enterprises (MSMEs). MSMEs play a pivotal role in the overall industrial economy of the country. In recent years the MSME sector has consistently registered higher growth rate compared to the overall industrial sector. The major advantage of the sector is its employment potential at low capital cost.

Definition:

In the Indian context, as per MSME Development Act, 2006, the micro, small and medium enterprises are defined *based on their investment in plant and machinery (for manufacturing enterprise) and on equipment for enterprises providing or rendering services.*

According to MSME Development Act, 2006, (India)

- A *micro enterprise* is where the investment in plant and machinery does not exceed 25 lakh rupees. In case of providing or rendering services the investment in equipment does not exceed 10 lakh rupees.
- A *small enterprise* is where the investment in plant and machinery is more than 25 lakh rupees but does not exceed 5 crore rupees. In case of providing or rendering services the investment in equipment is more than 10 lakh rupees but does not exceed 2 crore rupees.
- A *medium enterprise* is where the investment in plant and machinery is more than 5 crore rupees but does not exceed 10 crore rupees. And investment in equipment in service sector is more than 2 crore rupees but does not exceed 5 crore rupees.

Some of the major sub-sectors in terms of manufacturing output are- food products (18.97%), textiles and readymade garments (14.05%), basic metal (8.81%), chemical and chemical products (7.55%), metal products (7.52%), machinery and equipments (6.35%), transport equipments (4.5%), rubber and plastic products (3.9%), furniture (2.62%), paper and paper products (2.03%) and leather and leather products (1.98%).

Development and Administration of MSME:

The President under Notification dated 9th May 2007 has amended the Government of India (Allocation of Business) Rules, 1961. Due to this amendment, Ministry of Agro and Rural Industries (Krishi Evam Gramin Udyog Mantralaya) and Ministry of small Scale Industries (Laghu Udyog Mantralaya) have been merged into a single Ministry namely "Ministry of Micro, Small and Medium Enterprises (Sukshma Laghu Aur Madhyam Udyam Mantralaya)".

The administration of the MSME sector falls under the jurisdiction of the Ministry of Micro, Small and Medium Enterprises (MSMEs). It is the apex body to advise, coordinate and formulate policies and programmes for the development and promotion of the MSME sector. The office also maintains liaison with Central Ministries and other Central/State Government agencies/organisation, financial institutions.

Importance/Rationale of MSMEs:

The development of SME, i.e., Micro, Small and Medium enterprises sector is on the priority of Government Agenda.

As per the Results-Framework Document (RFD) for Ministry of Micro, Small and Medium enterprises (2012-13) the Mission of the Government is to: "promote growth and development of globally competitive Micro, Small and Medium Enterprises, including Khadi, Village and Coir Industries, in cooperation with concerned Ministries/Departments, State

Governments and other stakeholders by providing support to existing enterprises and encouraging creation of new enterprises, to endeavour to achieve a cumulative growth of 40%-50% in the number of registered enterprise by the end of 12th Plan and enhance this sector's *contribution to GDP* from the present 8%-10% by the end of the 12th Plan".

The role of MSMEs in *the economic and social development of the country* is well established. As per the Report of the Working Group on MSMEs growth for 12th Five Year Plan (2012-17), the sector accounts 45% of the manufacturing output and 40% of total exports of the country.

This sector *provides employment* to about 69 million persons through 26 million enterprises throughout the country.

Over 6000 *products ranging from traditional to high-tech items* are being manufactured by the MSMEs in the country.

The *labour to capital ratio in MSMEs* and the overall growth in the sector is much higher than in the large industries.

The geographical distribution of MSMEs is also even. Thus, MSMEs are important for the national objectives of *growth with equity* and inclusion.

Over the years, the small scale sector in India has progressed from the *production of simple consumer goods to the manufacture of many sophisticated* and precision products like electronics control systems, microwave components, electro medical equipments, etc.

The process of economic liberalisation and market reforms has further exposed these enterprises to increasing levels of *domestic and global competition.*

The MSME sector in India is *highly heterogeneous* in terms of the size of the enterprises, variety of products and services produced and the levels of technicians employed.

In short, MSMEs sector is being considered as the growth engine of any economy as it is characterised by their traditional strengths of relatively low investment requirements, effective resource utilisation, greater operational flexibility, mobility and higher innovativeness. It is true that developing countries face scarcity of capital and surplus of labour. More than 99% enterprises in European Union and near about 80% in USA are under this sector, and India is no exception.

In India,

- Its contribution towards balance regional development.
- Proper uses of local resources and talents.
- Remarkable contribution towards exports are about 40% of total export value and indirectly contributes 15% of export value.
- More than 95% industrial units belong to MSMEs sector and near about 45% industrial products are produced by this sector.
- Different categories of products and services are supplied by this sector and it ranges to more than 6000 different types.

- On an average 8% of GDP has been contributed by this sector and its share is rising upward and in near future if MSME are properly nurtured, it may cross agricultural sector's contribution which is at present about 15%.
- Its major contribution towards economy is in employment generation at low capital cost. The organised industrial sector requires an investment of ₹ 6.66 lakh to generate employment of one person, whereas the MSME sector generated employment of 1.27 persons with the same amount of investment.
- MSME sector is characterised by low investment requirement, operational flexibility and location-wise mobility.
- The sector has a high growth potential and performs a critical role in the manufacturing and value chains.

Weakness of MSMEs:
- While one end of the MSME spectrum contains highly innovative and high growth enterprises, more than *94% of MSMEs are unregistered*, with a large established in the informal or unorganised sector.

  As per the quick estimates of 4th All-India Census of MSMEs, the number of enterprises is estimated to be about 26 million and these provide employment to an estimated 60 million persons. Of the 26 million MSMEs, only 1.5 million are in the registered segment while the remaining 24.5 million (94%) are in the unregistered segment.
- The *state-wise distribution of MSMEs* show that more than 55% of these enterprises are in six states, namely, Uttar Pradesh, Maharashtra, Tamil Nadu, West Bengal, Andhra Pradesh, and Karnataka.
- Further, about 7% of MSMEs are owned by women and more than 94% of the MSMEs are proprietorships or partnerships.

Challenges to MSMEs:
Despite of the importance of the MSMEs in Indian economic growth, the sector is facing challenges and does not get the required support from the concerned Government Departments, Banks, Financial Institutions and Corporates which is proving to be a hurdle in the growth path of the MSMEs.

The major constraints being faced by the MSMEs in India are:
1. Problem in access is inadequate and timely finance on competitive terms, particularly the long term loans.
2. Difficulty in obtaining credit on easy terms and the resultant liquidity constraints in the Indian financial sector (due to global financial crisis) has held back the growth of MSMEs and impeded overall growth and development.
3. The financing constraints faced by this sector are attributable to a combination of factors that include policy, legal and regulatory framework (in terms of recovery, bankruptcy and contract enforcement), institutional weaknesses (absence of good credit appraisal and risk management and monitoring tools), and lack of reliable credit information on MSMEs.

4. Constraints of modernisation and expansion.
5. Non-availability of skilled labour at affordable cost.
6. Ineffective marketing strategy.
7. Low production capacity.
8. Lack of access to global market.
9. Complex labour laws and complicated procedures to compliance of such laws.
10. Issue relating to taxation and their procedure.
11. Problems of storage, packaging, product display etc.
12. Lack of marketing promotion both domestic and export
13. Lack of quality control and testing facility.
14. Non-availability of suitable technology.
15. Limited capital and knowledge.
16. Follow-up with various government agencies to resolve problems due to lack of manpower and knowledge, etc.
17. It has become difficult for lenders to be able to assess risk premiums correctly, creating differences in the perceived versus real risk profiles of MSMEs,
18. The sector has limited access to skilled manpower, R&D facilities and marketing channels.
19. In short, MSMEs lack availability of finance at cheaper rates, skills about decision-making and good management and accounting practices and access to modern technology.

Suggestions for Improvement

- **Providing Technology:** A number of appropriate technologies for the MSME sector have been developed in various sectors. Each MSME has its area of strength and weakness; hence it would be mutually valuable if the already developed technologies could be made available to each other. For this, a comprehensive list of all sorts of technologies should be prepared and made available according to the MSMEs requirement.

- **Providing Consultancy:** A list of experts and consultants should be prepared who can help the MSMEs within the region to effectively transfer the available technologies. These consultants could assist in market surveys, etc. Apart from assisting with the transfer, development and application of the technologies at a commercial level.

- **Dissemination of Information:** The slow intake in the utilisation of schemes is the lack of knowledge about schemes and their likely benefits. There is need to develop a better communication strategy and use of new age media tools like FM radio. Decision-making layers should not be more than two levels and should allow flexibility on operational issues.

- **Survey for Technological Needs:** Different surveys should be conducted to analyse the available technologies. These should also assess the availability of low-cost housing technologies, and alternative technology etc.
- **MSME Awareness of Government Initiatives:** There should be an information awareness campaign which identifies the Government's initiatives directed towards the assistance schemes, contribution, etc., through exhibitions, workshops, seminars, publication, etc.
- **Venture Capital:** There should be a sincere effort with a mutual exchange of views to overcome the venture capital problem. Study of venture capital availability and performance in relation to the country's technology development needs is obligatory. It involves the determination of the industrial investment on a sectoral basis and analysis of the role of venture capital in the investments made.
- **R&D Programmes:** There is an urgent need for the MSMEs to collaborate and adopt various R&D programmes. Hence it would be useful if there could be an exchange of views and information between the regions so as to overcome this problem.
- **Linkages:** There is a need to develop potential strategies in order to improve linkages and coordination between the Government, Industry and Academic.
- **Incubate new enterprises:** Each country should adopt certain appropriate mechanisms for technology business nurture in order to incubate new enterprises and provide technical advisory services to the MSMEs

To conclude, MSME sector shall grow significantly above the overall GDP growth in the country. The sector needs to adopt a proactive strategy approach where the government should propose a medium to long-term strategy to sustain themselves in the changing economic scenario and progress beyond the current GDP growth. Only with this the idea of pre-capital sector would be conceptualised in form of MSME sector. The crux solution to concentrate and flourish with the concept of pre-capital sector is *"enabling small business to grow big"*.

Points to Remember

- India started her quest for industrial development after 1947.
- The Industrial Policy Resolution of 1956 gave the public sector strategic role in the economy.
- The New Industrial Policy introduced a substantial programme of reregulation from public sector to private sector participation.
- Large scale industries refer to those industries which require huge infrastructure, man-power and have influx of capital assets.
- All the heavy industries in India like iron and steel industry, textile industry, automobile manufacturing industry fall under the large-scale industrial arena.
- The industrial structure has been widely diversified covering broadly the entire range of consumer, intermediate and capital goods.
- With industrial structure changes has been the emergence of a new progressing middle class of technicians, managers and entrepreneurs.

- The Industrial Policy Resolution of 1948 and 1956, the small sector was given special and significant role for creating additional employment with low capital investment.
- Small scale enterprises are classified as – Traditional small enterprises and Modern small enterprises.
- SSI's play a pivotal role in the Indian economy in terms of employment and growth.

Role of Public Sector :

(a) In critical areas.

(b) In export promotion.

(c) In import-substitution.

(d) In raising internal resources.

(e) In the growth of ancillary industries.

(f) In laying base of industrialisation.

(g) In infrastructure development.

(h) To the Exchequer of the Government.

(i) In employment.

(j) To GDP revenue.

(k) In savings and capital formation.

Problems of Public Sector :

(a) Under-utilisation of the installed capacity.

(b) Over-capitalisation.

(c) Political interference in location of industry.

(d) Inefficiency in management.

(e) Increase in construction cost due to delay.

(f) Inappropriate price policy.

(g) Heavy overhead expenditure.

(h) Excess use of man-power resources.

(i) Lack of co-ordination among different PSUs.

(j) Lack of research and Development.

Questions for Discussion

1. Discuss the problems of Public Sector in India.
2. Evaluate the role of public sector in Indian economy.
3. Discuss the role and importance of private sector.
4. Write in detail the role of public sector.
5. What do you mean by 'disinvestment policy'?
6. Write the challenges faced by MSMEs.
7. Discuss the role of MSMEs and the weakness of the sector.
8. Give the various suggestions to improve MSMEs.

■■■

Chapter **6**...

Industrial Imbalance

Contents ...

6.1   Introduction
6.2   Meaning of Industrial Imbalance
6.3   Need for Balanced Regional Development of Industries
6.4   Industrial Imbalance: Causes and Measures
6.5   Regional Industrial Imbalance: Special Focus on Maharashtra
   ➢   Points to Remember
   ➢   Questions for Discussion

Learning Objectives ...

At the end of the Chapter, you will be able:
* To learn about industrial imbalance
* To understand the need for balanced regional development of industries
* To be aware of the causes and measures of industrial imbalance
* To possess the knowledge of regional industrial imbalance with special focus on Maharashtra

6.1 Introduction

Any sound economic policy is important to economic development than mere expenditure of money by the Government. It is only by assessing the needs of the country, that a development plan could be made in the normal way.

In a planned economy, locational pattern of industries assumes a great significance as it helps in creating a climate for speedy development and acceleration of economic growth. Further, a balanced regional development of industries becomes necessary on social and economic grounds as also political, especially in a democratic country like India.

6.2 Meaning of Industrial Imbalance

Balanced regional growth is necessary for the harmonious development of a central State such as India.

India presents a picture of wide regional variations. Relatively speaking, some States are economically advanced while others are relatively backward.

Even within each State, some regions are more developed while others are almost primitive.

Regional imbalance implies co-existence of relatively developed and economically depressed States and even regions within each State.

> *Industrial imbalance is concentration of industries in certain regions and other regions have lesser number of industries and are therefore backward in development.*

As **R. Balakrishna** has pointed out, ".......... *fortuitous (unexpected or casual) circumstances have caused overdevelopment of industries in certain areas and have, therefore have not allowed ,under the capitalistic system, other areas from utilisation of their own natural resources for the production of commodities in the regions".*

As stated in the Sixth Plan (1980-85), "The fact that there are vast areas of the country which have remained backward over the years is both a challenge and an opportunity."

Table 6.1: Concentration of Large Scale Industries in Main Metropolitan Centres

Industries	Main Metropolitan Centres Which Witnessed Development
Textile Machinery	Ahmedabad, Baroda, Mumbai and Kolkatta.
Machine Tools	Bangalore and Pune.
Diesel Engines	Pune.
Railway Coaches	Chennai and Bangalore.
Electronics and Telecommunications	Bangalore and Hyderabad.
Defence Equipment	Kanpur and Pune.
Bicycle, Scooter and Motorcycles	Chennai, Mumbai, Delhi and Mysore.
Pharmaceuticals and Antibiotics	Trombay, Delhi, Pune and Mysore.
Electrical Goods	Mumbai, Kolkatta, Delhi, Chennai and Pune.

Table 6.1 depicts that many of the large-scale industries are concentrated in Mumbai, Pune, Kolkata etc. There is definitely an indication of disproportionate concentration of industries in a few cities. It generates a feeling that planning has made the rich richer and the poor poorer or the developed States becoming more developed and underdeveloped States remaining underdeveloped.

This fact can be depicted by State-wise contribution to Net Domestic Product (at constant price 1993-94).

Table 6.2: Statewise Net Domestic Product and Per Capita NSDP
(2004-05 to 2009-10) at 2004-05 prices

(₹ in Crores)

States	NSDP (₹ Crore)		Average Growth Rate	Per capita NSDP (₹)		Average Growth rate
	2004-05	2010-11		2004-05	2010-11	
Forward States						
Haryana	86,222	1,49,651	9.6	37,972	59,221	7.7
Punjab	86,108	1,29,933	7.1	33,103	44,752	5.2
Maharashtra	3,68,369	7,02,832	11.4	35,915	62,729	9.7
Gujarat	1,72,265	3,09,409	10.2	32,021	52,708	8.7
Andhra Pradesh	2,01,303	3,40,792	9.2	25,321	40,366	8.1
Karnataka	1,48,729	2,32,541	7.7	26,882	39,301	6.5
Backward States						
Assam	47,181	65,102	5.5	16,782	21,406	4.1
Rajasthan	1,12,636	1,78,184	8.0	18,565	26,436	6.0
Madhya Pradesh	99,940	1,60,549	8.2	15,442	22,382	6.4
Bihar	70,167	1,32,488	11.2	7,914	13,632	9.5

NSDP = Net State Domestic Product. Source: RBI, Hand Book of Statistics for Indian Economy (2010-11), CSO, National Accounts Statistics, 2011

- Reduction in regional inequalities is imperative not only from the point of view of improving living standards in backward states but also for faster economic development.
- The planning process, by helping the backward regions, made an effort to reduce regional disparities, but the forces of liberalisation and globalisation strengthened investment in forward states much more than in backward states.
- This widens the regional disparities due to industrial imbalanced development.

Table 6.3 : Growth Rate of State Domestic Product (SDP) in Different States

(in per cent)

Advanced States	VIIIth Plan	IXth Plan	Xth Plan	XIth Plan
Gujarat	12.4	4.0	10.6	9.6
Maharashtra	8.9	4.7	7.9	9.4
Goa	8.9	5.5	7.8	8.9
Kerala	6.5	5.7	7.2	8.0
Karnataka	6.2	7.2	7.0	8.0
West Bengal	6.3	6.9	6.1	7.3
Punjab	4.7	4.4	4.5	6.8

(in per cent)

Backward States	VIIIth Plan	IXth Plan	Xth Plan	XIth Plan
Chhattisgarh	N.A.	N.A.	9.2	8.4
Rajasthan	7.5	3.5	5.0	7.7
Jharkhand	N A	N A	11.1	7.0
Bihar	2.2	4.0	4.7	12.0
Uttar Pradesh	4.9	4.0	4.6	6.9
Madhya Pradesh	6.3	4.0	4.3	8.9

(N.A. = Not Available)

- Table 6.3 shows information about the growth rates of State Domestic Product during the 8th, 9th, 10th and 11th Plan for major States of India. With All-India average 7.6%, Punjab and west Bengal has been trailing behind and Gujarat indicated highest growth rate of 10.6%

- Though Jharkhand have indicated sharp increase in growth rate but otherwise there is a strong need to accelerate growth rate among the backward States so that regional disparity is reduced.

- From the above information presented, it is not only essential for speedy development and acceleration of economic growth but also necessary to highlight the need for dispersal of industries on strategic grounds. It is a parallel factor to meet the requirements of decentralised development of social and economic grounds.

India is a vast country with a variety of resources in different regions of the country. And, therefore, balanced regional industrial development should form an essential part of economic planning for the country. Balanced regional development is essential for providing employment opportunities to people in different regions, for reducing concentration of industries in certain regions and in a way help to reduce overcrowding, excessive pressure on housing accommodation, transport, health, water and educational facilities.

In fact, even with all the regulatory machinery for industrial planning in the country such as Industrial Licensing Policy, MRTP Act, Capital Issue Control, The Companies Act etc., excessive concentration of industries has been one of the serious defects of industrial growth in India, since 1950.

Balanced regional development does not mean that all regions in India should be developed industrially to the same extent. This is not possible as industrial resources are not evenly distributed in different regions of the country.

Further, balanced regional development must not also be misunderstood as encouragement to the spirit of provincialism or regionalism or regional self-sufficiency. This is neither desirable nor theoretically justified in a country like India.

Balanced industrial development implies maximum utilisation of available natural and human resources in the region to the extent possible by developing industries there on the basis of whatever resources are available in the region.

In India the territorial economic resources are unevenly distributed. The Regional Plans aim at a more and even development of the country. For example, power, mineral resources etc. which are essential for industrial development are most unevenly distributed. That is, some regions/areas are richer and some other regions relatively poor. As a result, lop-sided development is witnessed. To avoid this, the device of regional planning is resorted to ensure the consideration to the potentialities of each region.

The optimal industrial activity, based on sociological, economic and strategically consideration, is the main involvement of the regional development. As pointed earlier, regionalism is not provincialism or self-sufficiency as applied to the provinces.

The aim of regional development should be to secure maximum efficiency in the utilisation of available resources rather than adjustment of rival claims of different areas to achieve their own aims and ambitions. Thus, inter-provincial jealousy is detrimental to the execution of regional plan. Any conflict that may arise in the regional plans, which are complementary to the national plan, should be reduced in the interests of the progress of the nation.

Objectives of Regional Distribution of Industries:

India being vast country needs careful pattern of industrial development, so that each and every part of the country advances industrially forward.

Some of the objectives of regional distribution of industries are as follows:

1. In each region there are *certain local resources*. It is essential that these should be fully exploited to the advantage of the nation as a whole. Thus, for the proper utilisation of the resources and even development of local resources there is a need for dispersal of industries.

2. With the *dispersal of industries all over the country*, there is bound to be equilibrium of industrial development. In absence of such a development, there is bound to be inequalities; some regions having much more share than the other regions. It is regional development on rational basis, without creating feelings of provincialism, that equilibrium cam come in the society and in the country as a whole.

3. With imbalance in the regional development, people belonging to less developed regions *migrate to better developed regions*, thereby creating many social problems like the concentration of population, creation of slums, sanitation and civic amenities problems. Thus, the aim is avoidance of such problems.

4. In every region there are *certain resources which are likely to get exhausted*, in case these are not properly conserved. This can be made possible only by dispersal of industries in different regions and no region is ignored.

5. With equitable regional development, then people in each and every region will get an *opportunity to seek employment*. In such a case per capita income will increase and disparities, which are witnessed due to uneven distribution of income, are sufficiently reduced. But, in case balanced regional development of industries not cared for, there is bound to be wide gaps in the incomes of less developed and more developed industrially developed regions.

Indicators of Regional Imbalance:

For the study of regional imbalance some *forward states or advanced states* such as Punjab, Gujarat, West Bengal, Karnataka etc. and *backward states* like Madhya Pradesh, Assam, Uttar Pradesh, Rajasthan, Orissa and Bihar are considered.

1. The First Indicator that Depicts Regional Imbalance is Net State Domestic Product (NSDP). Punjab topped the list as it had the highest per capita income in 1990-91 and Orissa was at the bottom. However, in 2002-03, Maharashtra was at the top and Bihar was at the bottom on the basis of per capita income.

The average growth rate of net state domestic product of forward states was 6.03 per cent, while that of the backward state was only 2.69 per cent per annum.

Bihar indicated a distressing fact that there was negative growth rate of NSDP at (–) 0.99 per cent. Uttar Pradesh with a population of 166 million, it showed low growth rate of 2.79 per cent.

Madhya Pradesh depicted a dismal growth rate of 1.78 per cent of NSDP.

It indicates that the backward states – Uttar Pradesh, Bihar and Madhya Pradesh with a large population acted as a drag on the growth process of the Indian economy.

The planning process, by helping the backward regions, made an effort to reduce regional disparities, but the forces of globalisation and liberalisation have strengthened investment in the forward states much more than in the backward states. As a result, regional disparities have widened.

2. Growth Rates of State Domestic Product (SDP) in Different States: It gives information about the growth rates of SDP during the 8th, 9^{th,} 10th and XIth plan of major states of India (Refer Table 6.4).

Among the Forward States Gujarat indicated highest growth rate of 9.6% during the 11th plan. Punjab was on the top during 60's and 70's due to Green Revolution but has been trailing behind during the three plans in the range of 4.4 to 4.7%. West Bengal, Kerala and Andhra Pradesh showed lower growth rates than national average.

Among backward states Orissa, Chhattisgarh and Jharkhand showed a sharp increase in growth rates.

Madhya Pradesh and Bihar are still laggards in the growth process. There is a strong need to accelerate growth rate among the laggard backward states so that regional disparity is reduced.

3. Per Capita Net State Domestic Products: Another indicator of regional disparity is per capita net state domestic product (NSDP) at Constant Prices (1993-94).

Table 6.4: State-wise Per Capita NSDP

(₹ in Crores)

Forward States	1990-91	2004-05	Average Annual Growth Rates (1990-91 to 2004-05)
Punjab	11,776	16,756	2.5
Haryana	11,125	16,872	3.0
Maharashtra	10,159	17,864	4.1
Gujarat	8,788	16,878	4.8
West Bengal	5,991	12,271	5.3
Kerala	6,851	13,821	4.9
Tamil Nadu	7,864	13,999	4.2
Andhra Pradesh	6,873	12,352	4.3

(₹ in Crores)

Backward States	1990-91	2004-05	Average Annual Growth Rates (1990-91 to 2004-05)
Madhya Pradesh	6,350	8,238	1.8
Assam	5,574	6,721	1.4
Rajasthan	6,760	9,853	2.7
Uttar Pradesh	5,342	6,138	1.0
Orissa	4,300	7,176	3.7
Bihar	4,474	3,773	– 1.20
All India			3.4

Table 6.4 shows that in 1990-91 Punjab had the highest per capita income but in 2002-03 Maharashtra was at the top.

Orissa, in 1990-01 had lowest per capita income but in 2002-03 Bihar recorded the lowest per capita income.

Taking the 2 extremes – West Bengal recorded the highest annual average growth rate of per capital NSDP while Bihar recorded negative growth rate.

Advanced States thus register smart growth rate and backward states have registered extremely poor growth rates between 1 and 2.6 percent. This clarifies that backward states are not succeeding in catching up with forward states.

4. Trends in Investment and Financial Assistance in Regional Disparities: An extensive study on 'Widening Regional Disparities in India' by **Dr. N. J. Kurian** indicated that more than $2/3^{rds}$ of investment proposals (69.2 %) in the post-reform period were concentrated in the forward states.

Even the financial institutions distributed to forward states. For example, IDBI, IFCI, ICICI, UTI, LIC, IRBI, SIDBI disbursed 67.3 per cent of total financial assistance to forward states upto 31st March 1997. Four of the forward states namely Maharashtra, Gujarat, Tamil Nadu and Andhra Pradesh were able to appropriate 51 per cent of the total assistance.

This analysis clearly points out to the fact that the reform process has favoured the forward states in terms of approvals of investment proposals and in financial assistance. As a result, the already better-off states can further speed their growth process and there is retardation in backward states growth process.

5. Disparities in Infrastructure Facilities: Glaring infrastructure disparities are visible in India.

Consumption of **power per capita** is an indicator of level of energy consumption. States like Andhra Pradesh, Kerala and West Bengal - forward states – are above national average of 509 kwh. in 2007-08.

On the other hand, Bihar and Assam are way behind at 49 kwh. and 124 kwh. respectively.

Thus, unless the backward states, especially Uttar Pradesh industrialisation process picks up in these states, the disparities would continue. In fact even the reform process has sidelined these states.

Another indicator, though not very comprehensive indicator of the level of transport development is state-wise **number of registered vehicles** per 1000 persons. It is inadequate indicator as it does not take into account – railways and road length per 100 sq. kms. which has become major source of transport.

Not only registered vehicles per 1000 persons but even telecom lines per 100 persons is not a sufficient indicator. Because, the use of these criteria to indicate a direct connection between them and rate of development has its own limitations. Infrastructure development can be demand-driven when it is followed by investment in directly productivity activities. It is supply driven when it is preceded by investment in directly productive activities.

However, the development of infrastructure is an essential, though not a sufficient condition for development.

Infrastructure Development Index (IDI) developed includes following items with their weights :

(i)   Transport facilities   –   26 per cent
(ii)   Irrigation facilities   –   20 per cent
(iii)   Energy consumption   –   24 per cent
(iv)   Banking facilities   –   12 per cent
(v)   Communication facilities –   6 per cent
(vi)   Educational facilities   –   6 per cent
(vii) Health facilities   –   6 per cent

Taking the value of index for all India as 100, the relative values of IDI in the states indicate Punjab had the highest value of IDI as 191.4 and lowest value of IDI was for Madhya Pradesh (75.3), Assam (78.9) and Bihar (81.1).

Although Uttar Pradesh had a value of IDI (103.3) higher than all India level, yet in terms of poverty removal and food-grains production, it was far behind West Bengal, Tamil Nadu and Karnataka though having lower IDI values.

Irrigation infrastructure: Punjab had 95 per cent of irrigated area as a proportion of gross cropped area and thus topped in productivity per hectare.

On the other hand, Uttar Pradesh had, too, high irrigated area (63 per cent) but had relatively low productivity per hectare. This brings us to conclude that Punjab and Haryana were able to harness this high infrastructure facility for agricultural development.

6. **Social Infrastructure and Human Development:** Indicators of Human Development are – life expectancy, literacy rate, infant mortality rate, death and birth rate.

If the objective of all development is to improve quality of life, the human development indicators are the end-products of the development process.

Among different states, wide disparities have been observed. States like Kerala and to some extent Tamil Nadu have shown that it is possible to achieve higher level of human development even with low level of economic development.

To achieve higher levels of human development, it is necessary that investment in educational and health infrastructure is to be increased. Backward states like Bihar, Rajasthan and Uttar Pradesh have very poor record in terms of literacy (particularly female literacy). Further, these states have failed to step up investment in health infrastructure. As a result they exhibit lower life expectancy, higher infant mortality and higher birth rate.

The private sector has also shown disappointing results as in terms of welfare of the poor. The private sector which is torch-bearer of economic reforms do set up nursing homes and elite educational institutions that charge high fees but these meet the demand of the upper middle class and affluent sections and offer nothing for the welfare of the poor. Now, either the private sector should assume a higher social purpose or the state should invest more in educational and health infrastructure.

After a detailed analysis, Dr. **N. J. Kurian** of the Planning Commission concluded the following on regional disparities:

1. The accelerated economic growth since the early eighties with increased participation by the private sector appears to have aggravated regional disparities.

   The economic reforms since 1991, deregulation policies have been the prime instrument and have assisted the private sector resulting in increased inter-state disparities.

2. The better-off states are able to attract considerable amount of private investment – domestic and foreign – to improve their development potential. This is because these states have favourable investment climate including better socio-economic infrastructure. On the other hand, the backward states are unable to attract private investment because of unfavourable climate of investment and have poor infrastructure due to lack of resources. These backward states are in fact in a vicious circle. Investments are less attracted to these states due to poor infrastructure facilities and lack of resources is linked to their poor development.

3. During the planning process, there is evidence of the growth of regional disparities but still, the state made a conscious effort to reduce them.

But the reform process, which encouraged market forces within the country, together with globalisation favours the forward states and neglected the backward states. As a result, regional disparities increased.

6.3 Need For Balanced Regional Development of Industries

As compared to any other country in the world, India presents many problems of regional imbalances in development. There is inequitable growth of industrial areas or centres with a large cluster of large scale industries and the absolute negligence of a great part of the country.

In order that industrialisation may benefit the economy of the country as a whole, it is important that disparities in levels of development between different regions are progressively reduced.

The lack of industries in different parts of the country are often due to the factors such as non-availability of the raw material or other natural resources, non-availability or power, water supply and transport facilities which have not been developed there. Thus, one of the aims of the national planning is to ensure that these facilities are steadily made available to areas which are at present lagging behind.

Recognising the existence of these disparities in economic development of different States/Regions, the Industrial Policy Resolution adopted by the Parliament in 1956 and subsequent Resolutions, stressed the need of accelerated rate of economic growth and speedy industrialisation and removal of imbalances in the level of development between different regions/areas.

Industrialisation plays an important role in correcting the regional imbalances and accelerating the industrial growth. In order to remove regional inequalities and stimulate balanced industrial growth of different States/Regions, subsidies are given to industrial units that are set up in backward districts/non-industry districts.

While deciding on the locations of central public sector enterprises, due consideration is also given to backwardness of the regions.

Let us summarise the **need for balanced regional development of Industries in India:**

1. **For employment opportunities:** Regional development leads to the distribution of employment opportunities on an equitable basis. Such opportunities should not be confined only to a handful of States which are creating gaps in the per capita income among different regions.

2. **For national integrity:** Balanced regional development is also essential for national integrity. In other words, national integrity may be affected with the regional disparities in their prosperity.

3. **For planned utilisation of scarce resources:** It is of prime importance to any economy that there is planned utilisation and conservation of scarce and exhaustible in the interest of the nation. Thus, all efforts are directed towards the avoidance of

the destructive utilisation of resources i.e. coal, petroleum, forests etc. A neglect of this consideration has caused glaring differences in industrial progress of different provinces which are not always warranted by their natural conditions.

4. **To create privilege areas:** It has been observed that very fortunate circumstances have caused an over-development of industries in certain areas. As a privilege to the regional development through conservation of scarce resources of the country, the coking coal mines are nationalised in India and effective controls are laid on the consumption of petroleum.

5. **To achieve certain social objectives:** Through regional planning certain social objectives may be attained. It may include the removal of inequalities in the per capita income; it may lead to avoidance of migration of labour and may bring the uplift of backward regions. In short, regional planning is to arrest the growth of agglomerations which will create a few industrial centres or towns, which in their turn gives rise to housing problem, insanitary conditions, moral degradation, social problems etc.

6. **To maintain political stability:** Balanced regional development of industries is needed to maintain political stability in the country. Regional disparities in income and wealth are source of danger to national solidarity. This is what led to the formation of Bangladesh as an independent sovereign nation. Thus, the need to develop all regions equally stems from political and national solidarity.

7. **For national security**: Regional development is essential for a proper defence of the country from foreign attack. If all regions are equally developed and there is widespread dispersal of industries, the country can face all aerial attacks without much devastation. On the other hand, development of few regions and by concentration of industries can bring the entire economy to standstill in the event of its destruction by the enemy. Thus, for national security and defence, dispersal of industries is essential.

8. **For development of the economy as a 'whole':** Balanced regional development is essential for a rapid development of the economy as progress of the economy depends on the development of all regions keeping in view with their factor endowments. It is rightly said that "The progress of the national economy is reflected in the rate of growth realised by different regions". Greater development of resources in the regions must contribute towards accelerating the rate of progress for the economy as a whole.

9. **To minimise backwash effects:** Underdeveloped countries are featured by regional differences in income and employment. According to **Prof. Myrdal**, the main cause of regional inequalities has been the strong backwash effects and the weak spread

effects in such economies. The capitalist (private) system is guided by profit motive. Thus, development of those regions takes place where the profits are high while other regions remain underdeveloped.

Social and economic overheads get concentrated in certain regions leaving the rest of the country in a backwater. These inequalities are accentuated by migration, capital movements and trade. Migration of young and active people from the backward regions will favour the advanced region and depress economic activity in the backward regions. Capital will move into the developed regions thereby creating capital shortage in the backward regions.

The development of industries in developed regions may ruin the existing industries of the backward areas. So the backwash effects being stronger than the spread effects, regional inequalities are accentuated. Hence, the need in underdeveloped countries is to minimise the backwash effects through deliberate state action for a balanced regional development.

It has to be remembered that today's comparative advantage may not be a permanent one. Thus, there is a necessity of continuous persuasion for 'balanced growth' for diversification within considered limits.

6.4 INDUSTRIAL IMBALANCE: CAUSES AND MEASURES

Causes of Industrial Imbalance

- There are *certain deterrent factors* which come in the way of rapid development of a region; most important of these are the geographical isolation, inadequate economic overheads like labour, technology, transport etc.

- It is a historical fact that the existence of backward regions started with the *British rule in India*. They helped the development of only those regions which possessed facilities for prosperous manufacturing and trading activities. For example, the regions preferred by the British industrialists were Maharashtra and West Bengal. The main three metropolitan cities such as Calcutta, Bombay and Madras attracted all the industries and the rest of the country was neglected.

- On the rural scene, under *the land system of the British*, the rural areas were continuously pauperised and the farmers remained the most oppressed class. On the other hand, the money lenders and the zamindars were the prosperous ones. Thus, absence of effective land reforms presented disparities and became an obstacle to economic growth.

- In developing countries, *the developed regions are generally confined to urban centres*. This is mainly due to physical geography controls the economic growth in a greater degree in developing countries than in developed countries. For example, in developed countries like Japan and Switzerland, they have overcome the obstacles and constraints of mountain terrain but our Himalayan States such as Himachal Pradesh, Northern Kashmir, the hill districts of Uttar Pradesh and Bihar etc. have remained backwards and underdeveloped because of inaccessibility.

- *Climate* also plays a significant role in the low economic development of many regions in India as reflected in low agricultural output and absence of large-scale industry.

- *Location- wise some regions are preferred by the industrialists* because of certain locational advantages. For example, the location of iron and steel industries or oil refineries will have to be only in those technically defined areas, which are optimal to the industries. Naturally, as the process of development gain momentum, they attract labour, capital, trade and the external economies offered by the developing regions.

- New investments, in private sector, generally has a *tendency to concentrate in an already well developed area*, and thus tries to reap the benefits of external economies. This is an obvious tendency from the private investors as developed areas offer certain basic advantages such as labour, infrastructure facilities, transport and the market.

- Serious regional imbalances resulted during the *period of planned economic development* since 1950-51. The planning mechanism has encouraged the disparity between the States by having a strong favouritism favouring developed states and neglecting less-developed states. For example, Punjab and Haryana has always received the highest per capita plan outlays right from the First Plan to the Eighth Plan. At the same time, the poorest states like Bihar, Orissa, Uttar Pradesh and Rajasthan have received the smallest allocation per capita in all the plans.

- Again, since 1951, considerable investments have been concentrated at a few regions/towns like Mumbai, Delhi, Kanpur, Ahmadabad, Calcutta, Bangalore etc. on *'efficiency criteria'*. In fact, these areas have shown problems of congestion, slums, public health, transport etc. They have also caused serious resource and brain drain from the adjoining areas. In other words, when the growth centres experience cumulative and sustained economic growth, the neighbouring regions experience the flow of human, capital and other resources.

- During the 1960's with the adoption of new technology in agriculture, it increased economic disparities. Based on the assumption of using scarce resources most effectively and maximising food-grains production to solve the problem of food shortage, the Government concentrated its resources on farmers who enjoyed irrigated areas in different parts of the country. The already well-off farmers became better-off and the dry-land farmers and non-farming population of the countryside were neglected. This led to widening of the gap of income disparities between irrigated area and dry area farmers in every state.

- An attempt was made by the Government towards decentralisation and development of backward regions through public sector investment programmes in such areas as Bhilai, Rourkela, Barauni etc. But, the fact remains that the ancillary industries did not come up fast enough and these areas continued to remain backward despite heavy investment by the Centre.
- An additional cause for the growing regional imbalance is that some State Governments devoted much attention to the industrial development of their regions such as Punjab, Haryana, Gujarat, Maharashtra and Tamil Nadu, while others were more interested in political intrigues and manipulations than in rapid balanced economic growth of their areas.

The Industrial Licensing Policy Inquiry Committee appointed under the Chairmanship of **Mr. Dutt** commented that the Licensing Committee has failed in achieving the balanced regional development as the Licensing Committee granted licenses without paying any attention towards that objective.

The Committee further pointed out to the defect that the licensing authorities have been made helpless due to lack of specific plans for state-wise development of industries. The more advanced States received a larger number of licences. Further, the Committee also found that non-implementation of licences is more in backward states than in the highly advanced states. However, the Committee concluded that the Licensing Committee has shown a marginal regional growth in bringing about the dispersal of industries.

Measures to Correct Industrial Imbalance:

To tackle the problem of regional disparities in industrial development, the Planning Commission targeted at following policy measures:

1. Recognition of backwardness as a factor to be taken into account in transfer of financial resources from the Central Government to the States;
2. Special area development programmes directed at development of backward areas;
3. Measures to encourage private investment in backward areas.

At first we discuss the report of the Pande Committee.

The Pande Committee constituted by the Planning Commission in 1968 was to evolve criteria for the identification of backward areas in India. The first step towards the development of a backward region, it was the identification of backward areas. This Committee has laid down well-defined methods for identification of backward states and backward districts.

Following criteria has been laid down for identification of backward states and backward districts:

(i) Total per capita income;
(ii) The per capita income from industry and mining;

(iii) Number of workers in registered factories;

(iv) Per capita annual consumption of electricity;

(v)   Length of surfaced roads in relation to the population and the area of the state;

(vi) Railway mileage in relation to the population and the area of the state.

On the basis of the above criteria, the Committee identified the States of Andhra Pradesh, Uttar Pradesh, Assam, Jammu and Kashmir and Nagaland as backward.

The Committee recommended the following criteria for the identification of backward districts:

(i)   Districts beyond a radius of about 80 kms. to large cities or large industrial projects;

(ii)   Poverty as indicated by a low per capita income;

(iii) High density of population in relation to utilisation of productive resources and employment opportunities as indicated by:

(a) low percentage of population engaged in secondary and tertiary activities (25% below the state average may be considered as backward),

(b) low percentage of factory employment (25% below the state average as backward),

(c) low utilisation of economic and natural resources like minerals and forests; and

(iv) Adequate availability of electric power, transport and communications and water.

However, at the meeting of Chief Ministers with the Planning Commission, this distinction, as given by the Committee was not accepted. But it was agreed for the purpose of grant of incentives; those backward states should select two districts for development, whereas a developed state could select only one. In short, the limitation of available funds was obviously the deciding factor.

(i)   The Finance Commissions in India have used backwardness of a State as one of the criteria for the transfer of funds from the Centre to the States. The resource transfer refers to Central assistance for State Plans, i.e. *adhoc* transfers from the Centre to the States, distribution of assistance for centrally sponsored schemes, distribution of long-term and short-term credit from financial institutions etc.

In the First Plan central assistance provided to backward States was about 48 per cent, which increased to 57 per cent by the Third Plan. Since then there is a downward trend in the share of backward states in Central Plan assistance. For example, it was 50 percent during the Fifth Plan, 36 percent during the Sixth Plan and 37 percent in the Eighth Plan, showing a further decline to 36 per cent during the Tenth Plan.

There was a demand from many of the states to raise the allotment of central assistance to special projects from 10 percent to 25 percent, as suggested by Gadgil formula. This would benefit the backward states. However, even the revised formula for Central assistance could not benefit the backward states as intended. The basic difficulty highlighted in solving the regional imbalances and disparities through transfer of resources from Centre to States was that there was no guarantee that the resources transferred would be automatically utilised for the development of backward districts or regions. There was a tendency to divert such resources meant for backward areas to more advanced areas and for easier programmes.

(ii) With the help of Central assistance, Specific Plans have been made to develop the hilly, tribal and drought-prone areas. Various schemes were formulated for rural development that aimed at development of specific groups such as small farmers and agricultural labourers of backward areas. Later on these schemes became a part of block planning and for integrated rural development and full employment.

The Eleventh Finance Commission redefined the formula of transfer of resources from Centre to States. Along with other criteria, it included the relative distance of the per capita income of state with the income of the state with highest per capita income and infrastructure development index. Based on this new formula, backward states and special category states together would stand to receive 61.2 per cent of total resource transfer.

However, certain measures undertaken by the Centre indicates the intention of the Central Government to tilt the balance of allocations in favour of backward states. This is because the Central Government and the Twelfth Commission have made efforts to re-allocate resources to the benefit of the backward states. Out of the Normal Central Assistance, a forward state with a population of 52.5 percent would receive 44% of the funds. The Twelfth Commission allocated only 41% of the total funds to forward states. As a result, backward states with a population of 47.5 per cent received 56% funds from Normal Central assistance and the Commission allocated 58.6%.

(iii) Various incentives, both fiscal and others, have been provided by the Centre, States and by Public Sector Financial Institutions. These incentives aim at tackling the problem of industrial backwardness and promote private investment in backward areas.

Following are the various important incentives provided by the government of India to promote private investments in backward areas:

1. **Concession in Income Tax:** New industrial enterprises located in backward areas, set up after January 1971, are allowed a deduction of 20 percent of profits for computation of assessable income. This scheme of concession was introduced in April 1974 and was valid for a period of 10 years.

2. **Subsidised Transport:** The scheme of transport subsidy was introduced in July 1971. Industrial enterprises set up in hilly, remote and inaccessible areas were entitled to 50 percent transport subsidy on the expenditure incurred by them on raw materials transport and finished goods to and from certain selected rail heads to the location of the industrial unit. This scheme is applicable to Jammu and Kashmir and North-Eastern hilly regions.

3. **The scheme of Central Investment Subsidy:** This scheme was introduced in 1970. It provided for an outright subsidy at the rate of 10 percent and subject to a maximum of ₹ 5 lakhs on fixed capital investment, such as on land, buildings, plant and machinery. The subsidy was later raised to 15 percent and further to 20 percent. An exception was that the block/talukas/extensions of townships in Category B and C which have exceeded an investment ceiling of ₹ 30 crores at the end of March 1983 were to be excluded from the scope of the investment subsidy scheme.

    With effect from April 1984, electronics industrial units set up in hilly areas/districts would enjoy maximum limit of central investment of ₹ 50 lakhs (earlier it was ₹ 5 lakhs) at the rate of 25 percent as against 20 percent.

4. **Some other measures :** The Central Government has started a scheme of providing assistance to state governments in infrastructural development in identified 'no-industry districts' up to $1/3^{rd}$ (one-third) of the total cost of such development subject to a maximum of ₹ 2 crores. With this assistance from the Central Government, there has developed many growth centres through infrastructure development.

As mentioned above, it is together the Central Government, State Government and Public Sector Financial Institutions that have come forward with measures to favour the backward areas and set in a balance growth of the Indian economy. Now, we shall discuss the State help in correcting regional imbalances.

Incentives by State Government:

To attract private sector enterprises in the backward regions, state government has also offered many incentives.

These incentives include:

(i)   Providing developed plots with power and water on no-profit and no-loss basis;
(ii) Exemption from payments of water charges for few years;
(iii) Exemption from Octroi duties;
(iv) Exemption from payment of property taxes for few years;
(v)   Availability of interest-free loans on sales tax dues;
(vi) Preferential treatment for the purchase of stores for units located in backward areas;
(vii) Subsidy on industrial housing scheme etc.

The studies show that in recent years more than fifty percent of the assistance in terms of financial schemes sanctioned by SFC's, SIDCO, and SIICs have been provided to districts designated as backward.

Assistance by Major Financial Institutions:

Industrial Development Bank of India (IDBI), the Industrial Finance Corporation of India (IFCI) and the Industrial Credit and Investment Corporation of India (ICICI) are the major Public Sector Financial Institutions. They provide concessional finance for industrial projects located in backward areas.

The concessions are as follows:

(i)   Lower rate of interest on rupee loans for example, 9.5 per cent as against 11.5 percent,

(ii) A longer period of repayment for example, 15 to 20 years as against 10 to 12 years,

(iii) Charging half the normal rate of underwriting commission,

(iv) Participation in the risk capital or debenture issues, waiving of commitment charges etc.

Certain other constructive and helpful steps taken by these three financial institutions are preparing at their own cost feasibility study projects which seem promising. They encourage prospective entrepreneurs to assess them and take interest in implementing them.

Entrepreneurial training programmes are conducted for the benefit of small and medium entrepreneurs.

IDBI has been instrumental in setting up several technical consultancy organisations throughout the country. The technical consultancy services provided are so very necessary for the development of the backward areas.

Tenth Plan Strategy (2002- 2007):

Every five year plan has shown widening disparities between states and regions. Equally true is the fact that these disparities have to be narrowed down. The Tenth Plan took up this problem as a challenge, as these backward regions have continued to be 'high poverty, low growth and poor governance' despite best of efforts put in the government.

It is well known that states/regions with developed infrastructure attract private investment in much larger measure than other states/regions. Thus, the Tenth Plan would like to adopt a strategy to accelerate the development of less developed states and backward regions within the developed states. The strategy of the Tenth Plan is as given under:

1. A high proportion of central assistance and States own resources would be devoted in improving infrastructure gaps in less developed states.

2. Development efforts should be accompanied by Governance and institutional reforms to make the investments/resources provided by the centre and state more effective.

Based on this strategy, the Tenth Plan formulated a new scheme called Rashtriya Sam Vikas Yojana (i.e. National Equal Development Plan) to support the development initiative in backward states and regions. This scheme was introduced in the year 2002-03, and focus on helping the backward areas to overcome poverty and unemployment. The scheme would facilitate the states to take up productivity-enhancing reforms. The reforms are in the administrative and financial structure, the manner in which the financial and administrative powers are delegated and include policies relating to the day-to-day life of the ordinary people. Further, the reforms undertaken should have a multiplier effect on the concerned regions.

The report of the previous plan years showed that not only there was bottleneck of funds in the development process, but the existing rules and the manner in which they are interpreted prevent the services meant for the poor and other target groups.

Under the present scheme of National Equal Development Plan, each state has to identify and choose the reforms process and enter an agreement with the Centre to implement the reform process. Only those states which enter into such agreement would stand to benefit and would receive funds based on **Gadgil-Mukherjee Formula**.

Eleventh Five Year Plan and Balanced Regional Development:

In the Eleventh Five Year Plan commenting on regional imbalances, the statement given therein is, "Redressing regional imbalances has indeed been a vital objective of the planning process. However, despite the efforts made, regional disparities have continued to grow and the gaps have been accentuated as the benefits of economic growth have been largely confined to better developed areas. With the removal of controls and the opening up of the economy to external forces, the pressure of market forces may tend to exacerbate inter and intra-state disparities."

The Plan also mentions that redressing regional disparities is not only the goal in itself but it is also essential for maintaining social and economic integration, without which the country may be faced with a situation of discontent, anarchy and breakdown of law and order.

The schemes and programmes in the Plan are targeted towards poor areas and poor people especially those below the poverty line. And, since the backward regions have population more of poor people, their share in the schemes is bound to be more.

Strategy for Development of North-Eastern Regions:

States like Arunachal Pradesh, Assam, Manipur, Mizoram, Meghalaya, Nagaland, Sikkim and Tripura constitute North-Eastern region. These States have been classified as **Special Category States.** Only after the formation of North-Eastern Council, these states received special attention.

During the first two decades of planning, these states did not participate in the process of planned development and were thus deprived of the benefits of infrastructure development. However, during 1973 and 2006-07, a total investment of ₹ 7,182 crores has been made in North-Eastern Region (NER). Out of this, 46.7% (i.e. ₹ 3,315) was used for the development of transport and communications. Further, ₹ 2,586 crores i.e. 36% was utilised for power and water. It can be said that 83% of total investment is on the abovesaid items and meagre share left for development in agriculture, industry and human resource.

The Eleventh Plan comments that since the non-renewable resource such as coal is expected to be exhausted during the next 30 years, it would be desirable to take up hydro-power projects in NER (NER has great potential in hydro-power of 62.357 MW i.e. 42.5% against All-India potential of 1,48,702 MW). These projects would not only benefit the whole country but also reduce the disruption in communication and loss of life and property due to frequent occurrence of floods and landslides in NER. During the period of 2002-2007 a total investment of ₹ 80, 940 were made in the NER.

As stated by the Eleventh Plan, the NER is rich in development in terms of human resource and natural resources, but for the lack of infrastructure growth is stunted in this region. The primary sector has remained largely stagnant; the manufacturing sector has been handicapped due to various reasons. Thus, there is a need to encourage and focus on the growth of agriculture and industry in NER.

We summarise, in general, some steps for regional development of industries:

1. Political division of the country should be on such rational basis that each unit become economically self-sufficient. Each unit should have economic and natural resources for growth and development and should be dependent on other regions to the extent possible.

2. Many a times while deciding about location of industries, political pressures may be exerted. It is therefore, very essential that economic influence and not political pressure should decide the location of industrial unit.

3. As an outcome to the above point, it is essential to ensure that new industries are located in regions that are backward and not encourage units in already developed areas.

4. Due importance should be given to cottage and small scale industries, as they have the potential to correct regional disparities and are conducive to the Indian economy, which suffers from chronic unemployment and slow rate of capital formation.

5. Each Plan should aim at developing infrastructural facilities and industrial estates in different states to encourage private investments and over-all development of that region/state.

6. It is very essential that proper research studies should be conducted to find out the industries where there are chances of decentralisation. Decentralisation would shift industrial units from congested areas to industrially backward areas.

7. Each region is endowed with natural resources and as such with raw material to industries. It is thus essential to set-up industries as raw-material oriented and is also economically viable.

8. For proper development of each region, it is necessary that Planning Boards are constituted. These Boards can function at zonal level and is in close co-operation with the planning commission. The Boards can look into the following matters :
   - Prepare comprehensive development plan of the region, after taking into consideration the available economic and natural resources, available man power, transport and other facilities.
   - It should recommend, whether the region is more suitable for the growth of heavy, cottage or small-scale industrial units, capital goods or consumer goods industries.
   - It should prepare a plan on provision of housing and other civic amenities in the event of industrial development.
   - It should provide technical knowledge and adequate data and information about the location of industries to potential entrepreneurs and industrialists, to encourage their investments in that region.

Certain positive and negative approaches to bring about regulation in the location of industries can be adopted by the state to correct the lopsided development in different regions.

For proper regional development and industrial growth of the nation as a whole, some measures can be taken to regulate industrial location. These can be of positive approach and of negative approach. By positive approach we mean ways in which the state provides an encouragement and negative approach is when the state can put in some deterrents to setting up of industries in particular area/region.

In positive measure for regional development incentives are provided in various forms – better public utility services like transport, water supply, power, marketing organisation, socio-economic facilities, basic data of the region, potential growth of the region etc. Similarly, industries desired to be located in a particular area can be provided subsidiary facilities, directly or indirectly. Industries can be provided loans at lower rate of interest, tax reliefs on commodities manufactured by those units etc.

An encouraging measure can be that the state assures such industries that the Government will be willing to purchase their products. The state can also help the units in procuring order for them even across the country. The government may announce incentives to industrial enterprises, those willing to set up in industrial estates. In fact, setting up of industrial estate may be a boon to that region's development.

The negative measures should not be understood as obstacles to the development of industries. These measures are more aimed at dispersal than hampering the growth of industries. In the broader sense it can be said that by providing incentives to an industry in one area is like creating deterrent for the same industry if set up in other areas.

The negative approach of the state may be in the form of relative heavy taxes on particular industrial products produced by an industry in a particular area. To avoid concentration of industries in a particular area, certain levies can be imposed on new industrial units. New industrial licences may not be issued to the industry in that particular area.

Wanchoo Committee:

The Wanchoo Committee recommended the following fiscal incentives for industries set up in backward areas:

(i)   Grant of higher development rebate;

(ii)   Exemption from income tax, including corporate tax, for five years, after providing the development rebate;

(iii) Exemption from import duties on plant and machinery and components;

(iv)   Exemption from excise duties for five years;

(v)   Exemption from sales tax both on raw materials and finished products for five years from the date of going into production;

(vi)   Grant of transport subsidy for the despatch of finished products for five years. There would be no subsidy up to a distance of 640 kms. and the subsidy has been recommended only in areas of difficult communications.

The Central Government on the recommendations of the Pande Committee and the Wanchoo Committee announced two schemes in 1971 for providing financial assistance and transport subsidy to the entrepreneurs intending to set up industries in selected backward areas. The Central Government notified many districts eligible for financial concessions. The IDBI, IFCI and ICICI extended concessional rupee loan assistance to new concerns setting up projects in specified backward regions, irrespective of their project cost. Concessional finance for expansion/diversification projects in identified backward districts undertaken by existing concerns would be considered on selective basis, keeping in view the profitability potential of the existing and proposed new projects, location of new projects and other related factors.

In August 1975, an 11-member committee under the chairmanship of the then Secretary of Industries, Government of Maharashtra, **Shri P. C. Nayak**, was constituted to examine the question of development of backward areas. This Committee suggested a five-fold strategy of backward areas development.

1. Setting up of a central authority to be called 'Authority for Backward Area Development (ABAD), at national level. Its function is to assist in planning, sponsoring and promoting a co-ordinated programme for the speedy industrial development of backward areas.

2. To use the close link between urbanisation and industrialisation for promoting development of these areas. Suitable 'growth centres' are to be selected with potential for development. All efforts then should be concentrated on such growth centres for promoting large and medium industrial units, so that within a period of five years, concrete results can be achieved. It strongly recommended that a system of disincentives should be adopted by the Union Government to ensure that large metropolitan centres do not attract large and medium industries.

3. It suggested adopting an 'approach for balanced development of large, medium and small industries'. Large and medium industries necessarily need physical and social infrastructure at growth centres, but small scale industries can have a wide spread impact on geographical dispersal of industries.

   Thus, the total number of growth centres to be taken up for development of large and medium industries, during the next five years, have necessarily to be limited to a manageable number for getting desirable and concrete results. On the other hand, there should be no such restriction for a widespread growth of small-scale industries in the entire backward areas. It would encourage development of local entrepreneurship. The large and medium industries would encourage, with time, the development of ancillary industries in the hinterland.

4. The next strategy was to bring about organisational and administrative measures to ensure that all backward areas get uniform advantage of present schemes operated by the union Government.

5. Better rearrangement and realignment of the existing schemes should be made so that better results are obtained quickly.

The Industrial Policy statement of 1977 attaches great importance to the balanced regional development of the entire country so that disparities and levels of development between regions are progressively reduced. It stated that the government has noted with concern that most of the industrial development that has taken place in our country since Independence has been concentrated around the metropolitan areas and large cities. As a result it has led to rapid deterioration in the living conditions especially for the working class in the larger cities and has given rise to slums and environmental pollution. So, the government has decided that no more licences should be issued to new industrial units.

Within certain limits of large metropolitan cities having a population of more than 5 lakhs as per the 1971 census, it recommended that the state governments and financial institutions to deny support to new industrial units in these areas. The Government of India promised to consider providing assistance to large existing industries which wanted to shift from congested metropolitan cities to approved location in backward areas.

With the announcement of incentives for setting up industries in 'no-industry districts/backward areas', the Central Government amended the Central Investment Subsidy Schemes during 1982-83. The backward districts in the country were classified into three categories for Central Investment Subsidy Scheme.

- **Category A (188 districts) :** 25 percent of the fixed capital investment or additional fixed capital investment, as the case may be, subject to a maximum of ₹ 25 lakhs.
- **Category B (55 districts) :** 20 percent of fixed capital investment or additional fixed capital investment, as the case may be, subject to a maximum of ₹ 20 lakhs.
- **Category C (113 districts) :** 15 percent of fixed capital investment or additional fixed capital investment, as the case may be, subject to a maximum of ₹ 15 lakhs.

The Companies registered under the MRTP Act, 1969 and FERA 1974, will not be eligible for Central Investment Subsidy Scheme in 'C' category.

The industrial units coming up in block/taluka/urban agglomerations, extension of township in Category B and C, where investments had exceeded ₹ 30 crores, as on the 31st March, 1983, shall, however, not be eligible for Central Investment Subsidy.

Keeping in view the need for developing backward areas and the role played by MRTP and FERA companies, Government have also decided to permit entry of these companies into industries not reserved for small-scale sector, with an export obligation of 4 percent for setting up industries in Category B and C districts and 30 percent in respect of Category A districts.

Additional concessions would be provided by the government to certain industrial units identified by central subsidy districts as nucleus plants which would be expected to promote new ancillaries in the local areas, as part of their programme of 50 percent ancillarisation.

To conclude, in recent years, the problems associated with industrial location have received closer attention and acquired great importance than ever before. Concentration of a large number of industrial units, producing a similar kind of goods at a place, has led to many problems of housing, transport, and other social services. Therefore, decentralisation or dispersal of industries has become the need of the hour, to achieve balanced regional development.

6.5 Regional Industrial Imbalance: Special Focus on Maharashtra

"The co-existence of relatively developed and economically depressed States and even regions within each State is known as Regional Imbalance".

One of the reasons of regional industrial imbalance is due to *"neglect of some regions and preference of others for investment and development efforts".*

Maharashtra State was created on the 1st May 1960 with the merger of two Marathi speaking areas of Marathwada and Vidarbha. The present state of Maharashtra comprises of three regions, namely, (1) Rest of Maharashtra (ROM- Western Maharashtra, Konkan and Mumbai City); (2) Vidarbha; (3) Marathwada.

New Economic Policy (1991)

The impact of liberalisation, privatisation and globalisation on backward areas like Vidarbha and especially Marathwada has been quite adverse. Table 6.5, explains the development of industrial sector (1991 – 2009).

Table 6.5: Development of Tiny, Small and Medium and Large Scale Industries in Maharashtra (as on 30th Nov., 2009), (in percentage)

Region	No. of Tiny, Small, Medium Enterprises	Employment	Large-scale Units	Employment
Rest of Maharashtra (ROM)	76.9	75.3	83.6	79.6
Marathwada	7.7	8.6	5.3	6.6
Vidarbha	15.4	16.1	11.1	13.8

Source: "Economic Survey of Maharashtra-2009-10, Government of Maharashtra Mumbai, p.101

- This table shows that between 1991 and 2009 ROM region has made phenomenal industrial progress, due to its location advantage and better infrastructure facilities in this region.
- About 3/4th of the total industrial units are located in this region while, of the total industrial employment about 80% is created in this region.
- The position of Marathwada is extremely poor, both in terms of proportion of industrial units (7% to 8%) and employment (5% to 6%) during this period.
- The position of Vidarbha is little better in terms of industrial units (15%) and employment (13% to 16%).
- This clearly shows a very lopsided industrial development of the State, which may be considered as a major factor leading to rising regional disparities in the State.

Table 6.6: Progress of Special Economic Zones (SEZs) (upto 2009 in Maharashtra), in Percentage

Region	No. of SEZ	Proposed Investment	Employment
ROM	82.6	90.7	88.8
Marathwada	10.4	6.6	2.3
Vidarbha	7.0	2.7	8.9

- Even in case of SEZs in Maharashtra shows that more than 80% SEZs are located in ROM.
- In terms of proposed investment 90% is to be made in ROM, creating 90% of total employment.
- Due to poor infrastructure facilities in the other two regions, the proposed investment and employment created is extremely poor.
- If the present situation continues, the regional disparities are bound to increase.

Institutional Structure and Industrial Development

Due to the existence of the historically developed industrial centre of Mumbai and the strong pull it exerts, the regional disparities in matter of industrial development are some of the acutest in Maharashtra. In 1974, the State Government and the City of Industrial Development Corporation of Maharashtra (CIDCO) commissioned Tata Consultancy Services to undertake a study of Industrial location in Maharashtra.

- The State Government created two major institutions for promoting industrial development in the State, particularly in underdeveloped and developing areas. The MIDC (Maharashtra Industrial Development Corporation) set up in 1962 with the objective of securing and assisting rapid and orderly establishment and growth of industry in the State. The MIDC develops industrial areas in different parts of the State and provides industrial plots and sheds along with requisite infrastructure in roads, water and power and other common facilities.
- The other institution is the SICOM (State Industrial and Investment Corporation of Maharashtra) set up in 1966 mainly to promote industrial development in the underdeveloped areas of the State. For SICOM to focus its efforts on underdeveloped areas, Bombay Metropolitan Region and Pune Metropolitan Region are kept out of its jurisdiction.
- The SICOM provides wide ranging facilities and concessions to entrepreneurs intending to set up industrial units in the developing areas of the State.
- Other important State level agencies are the Maharashtra Small Scale Industries Development Corporation (MSSIDC) set up in 1962. Its major function is to procure and distribute raw materials to the registered small-scale industries.
- There are four regional development corporation for Marathwada, Vidarbha, western Maharashtra and Konkan respectively. These are expected to attend to the overall development of their region, with major focus on industrial development. They are expected to play a catalytic role and co-operate the activities of the various state level corporations and government agencies working in their regions.

How to reduce Industrial Imbalance in State of Maharashtra?

1. To reduce inter-district disparities the classification of districts into "backward" and "developed" is important which was earlier avoided.

2. By identifying "backward" and "developed" regions/districts, we could design policies for the accelerated development of backward districts by providing additional funds to these districts. Unless backward districts are provided higher level of investment than the "developed" districts, the objective of reducing regional disparities cannot be achieved.

3. The additional funds should be utilised in each of the identified backward districts through SWOT analysis and 'vision documents' of each district, so that full potential of each district is exploited.

4. The State Planning Board had appointed a Committee in 1992 to identify the backward areas in Maharashtra State. The committee identified 17 districts in Maharashtra as backward by using 12 socio-economic indicators. These districts are:-
   - Vidarbha 8 districts- Gadchiroli, Buldhana, Amravati, Chandrapur, Yavatmal, Akola, Bhandara, Wardha.
   - Marathwada 6 districts – Jalna, Parbhani, Osmanabad, Latur, Beed, Nanded.
   - ROM 3 districts – Dhule, Ratnagiri, Sindhudurg.

5. The Committee suggested 15% of the Plan Funds for accelerated development of these 17 districts based on their population.

To conclude, a balanced regional development of industries becomes necessary on social and economic grounds as also political, especially in a democratic country like India.

Points to Remember

- In a planned economy, locational pattern of industries assumes a great significance.
- A balanced regional development of industries becomes necessary on socio-economic and political grounds in a country like India.
- Regional imbalance implies co-existence of relatively developed and economically depressed states and even regions within each state.
- Industrial imbalance is concentration of industries in certain regions and other regions have lesser number of industries and are therefore backward in development.
- Balanced regional development is essential:
  (i) for providing employment opportunities to people in different regions;
  (ii) for reducing concentration of industries in certain regions and
  (iii) to avoid congestion in those areas.
- Balanced regional development does not mean that all regions in India should be developed industrially to the same extent.
- Balanced industrial development implies maximum utilisation of available natural and human resources in that region.

Objectives of Regional Distribution of Industries:

- Optimum utilisation of local resources.
- Dispersal of industries to bring equilibrium of industrial development.
- Avoid social problems like creation of slums, sanitation etc.
- Prevent indiscriminate use of certain resources by encouraging dispersal of industries in different regions.
- More equitable distribution of income.

Need for Balanced Regional Development of Industries:

- To promote balanced regional development.
- To achieve accelerated rate of economic growth in different regions.
- Increase employment opportunities, growth of small-scale and ancillary units etc.

Causes of Industrial Imbalance:

- Development of those areas which possessed facilities for prosperous manufacturing and trading activities.
- Developed regions confined to urban areas due to physical geography controls, for example, in hilly districts development is poor.
- Industries are set up to the location wise advantages for example, where there is existence of external economies.
- Planning mechanism has encouraged the disparity by favouring developed states.
- Few state governments devoted attention towards industrial development of their regions; others were more interested in political intrigues and in less important issues.

Measures of Industrial Imbalance:

- Identification of backward areas to transfer financial resources from the Central Government to states.
- Measures to encourage private investment in backward areas.
- Special area development programmes directed at development of backward areas.
- Announcement of various incentives by the government.
- Incentives by State Government and Public Sector Financial Institutions.

Questions for Discussion

1. What do you understand by 'regional imbalance'?
2. Give detailed information on 'industrial imbalance' in India. Support your answer with statistical data.
3. Mention the objectives of regional distribution of industries.

4. Give arguments in favour of balanced regional development of industries.

5. Discuss the various causes leading to industrial imbalance in Indian Economy.

6. What are the measures towards correction of industrial imbalance?

7. Suggest the measures regarding correction of industrial imbalance as given by the Planning Commission.

8. What are the different indicators of regional disparities?

9. Discuss the need for Balanced Regional Development of Industries.

■■■

QUESTION PAPERS
April 2012

Time: 3 Hours   Max. Marks: 100

Q.1 State and explain scope and significance of Industrial Economics.   **[20]**
                                    OR
Q.1 Critically examine Weber's Theory of Location of Industries.   **[20]**
Q.2 What is Industrial Productivity? Explain factors affecting Industrial Productivity.   **[20]**
                                    OR
Q.2 State and explain progress and problems of Public Sector.   **[20]**
Q.3 Critically examine role and problems of Special Economic Zone.   **[20]**
                                    OR
Q.3 What are the causes of Industrial Imbalance in India?   **[20]**
Q.4 State and explain impact of Industrialisation on Urbanisation.   **[20]**
                                    OR
Q.4 State and explain problems of Small Scale Industries in India.   **[20]**
Q.5 Write short notes: (Any Two)   **[20]**
   (a) Sergeant Florence's Theory of Location of Industries.
   (b) Need of Balanced Regional Development.
   (c) Impact of Industrialisation on Global Warming.
   (d) Relationship between Industrial Development and Economic Development.

■■■

October 2012

Time: 3 Hours   Max. Marks: 100

Q.1 Explain scope and significance of the Study of Industrial Economics. [20]
                                    OR
Q.1 Explain impact of Industrialisation on Global Warming.   **[20]**
Q.2 Discuss Weber's Theory of Location of Industries.   **[20]**
                                    OR
Q.2 Explain need of Balanced Regional Industrial Development.   **[20]**
Q.3 What is Industrial Productivity? Explain factors affecting Industrial Productivity.   **[20]**
                                    OR
Q.3 Explain role and problems of Public Sector in India.   **[20]**
Q.4 Critically examine role and problems of Special Economic Zones (SEZ).   **[20]**
                                    OR
Q.4 What are the causes of Industrial Imbalance in India?   **[20]**
Q.5 Write short notes: (Any Two)   **[20]**
   (a) Sergeant Florence's Theory of Industrial Location
   (b) Measurement of Industrial Productivity
   (c) Impact of Industrialisation on Urbanisation
   (d) Problems of Small Scale Industries

■■■

April 2013

Time: 3 Hours   Max. Marks: 100

1. State and explain scope of Industrial Economics.   [20]

OR

State and explain inter-relationship between industrial development and economic development.   [20]

2. State and explain factors influencing on Location of industries.   [20]

OR

What is Industrial Productivity? Explain factors influencing on Location of industries.   [20]

3. State and explain role and problems of public sector in India.   [20]

OR

State and explain role and problems of small scale industries in India.   [20]

4. State and explain causes of Regional industrial imbalance in India.   [20]

OR

Explain Weber's theory of industrial location.   [20]

5. Write notes on (any two):   [20]
   1. Significance of Industrial Economics.
   2. Sargent Florence's theory of location of industries.
   3. Role of private sector industries in India.
   4. Importance of Industrial Regional Development.

■■■

April 2015

Time: 3 Hours   Max. Marks: 50

1. State and explain scope and limitations of Industrial Economics.   [14]

OR

State and explain Sarjent Florences theory of location of Industries.

2. What is Industrial productivity? Explain factory influencing on Industrial Productivity.   [14]

OR

Explain measures adopted by Indian Government to improve Industrial Efficiency.

3. (a) Explain functions of private sector enterprises.   [7]
   (b) Explain problems of public sector enterprises.   [7]

OR

   (a) Explain problems of small and medium enterprises in India.
   (b) Explain effects of industrial imbalance.

4. Write short notes (any two):   [8]
   (a) Relationship between Industrial development and Economic development.
   (b) Causes of Industrial imbalance.
   (c) Measurement of Industrial Profitability.
   (d) Disinvestment policy.

■■■